I0552318

Copyright © 2019 by Camille Douglass
All rights reserved.
Cursed Lines
First Publication: February 2019
Dead Mouse on Cheese Publishing
ISBN: 978-1-950163-02-1 (ebook)
ISBN: 978-1-950163-03-8 (paperback)

Cover Art: Deranged Doctor Design

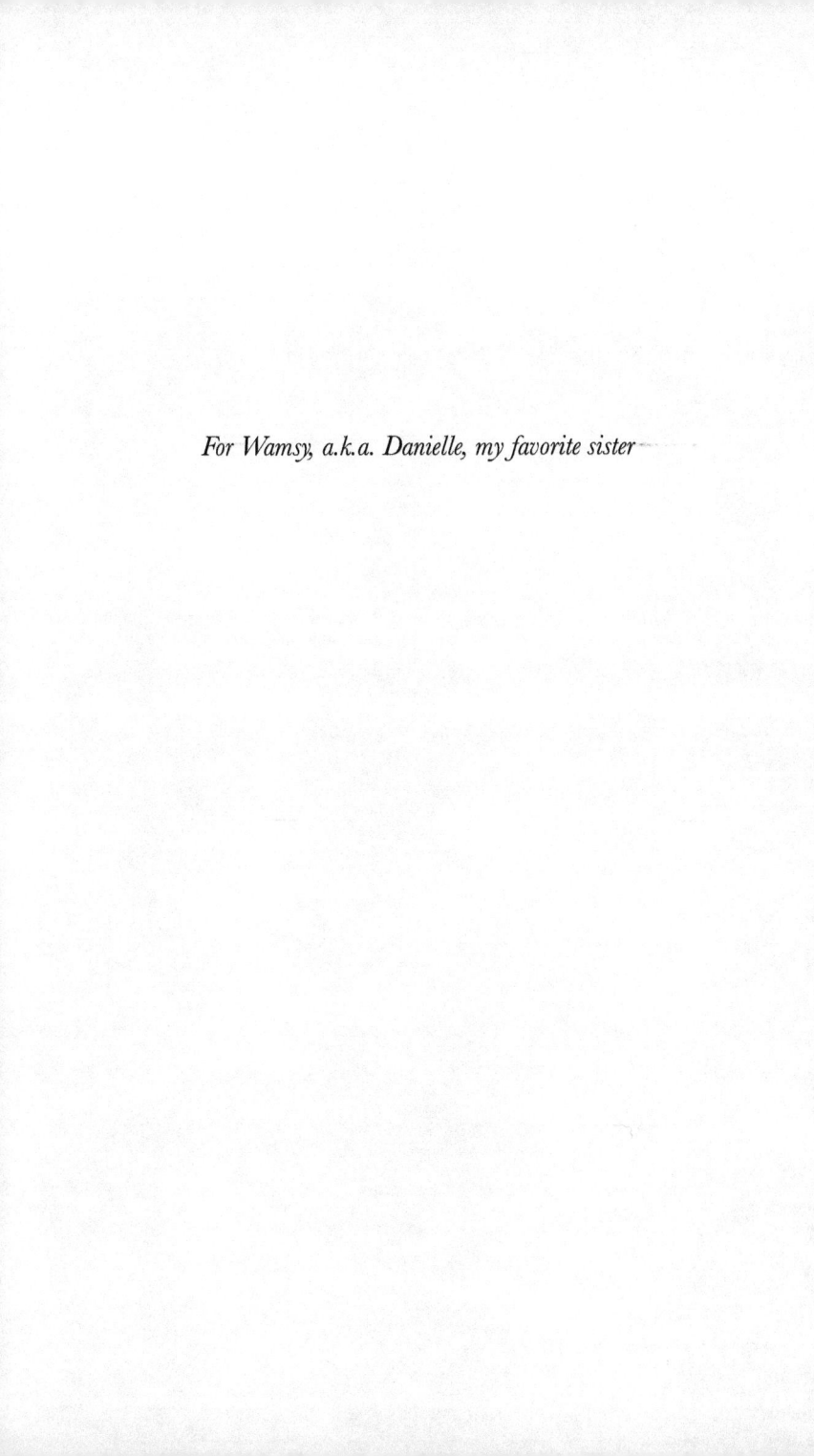

For Wamsy, a.k.a. Danielle, my favorite sister

ACKNOWLEDGMENTS

It takes an oddly functioning village of your own creation. I have many people to thank in said village. Thank you to my family, I could not have asked for a better one. We're crazy but the good kind. My friends, you embrace the above mentioned crazy. Jessica from Red Adept Editing. You make my writing much tighter and stop me from making massive historical errors. Any other errors are my own. Deranged Doctor Design, you make pretty covers. Finally, to the readers who have embraced this series: thank you, thank you, thank you!

A PEG DARROW NOVEL

CURSED LINES

CAMILLE DOUGLASS

1
_____

"Seriously? You expect me to put a black sack on my head and let you drive me to gods know where?" I stifled a yawn, hiding it behind my hand as I leaned against the doorjamb of my front door.

"The queen requires you. This is a normal security procedure." The goblin woman in front of me was probably aiming for cajoling, but all I heard was annoyed.

The feeling was mutual.

"I get that, I really do, but I just got home from Boot Camp. Even my pinkies hurt. Did you know that finger muscles could hurt?" After six weeks at a Mercenary Boot Camp for witches and a flight from Chicago, my plan for the evening included pizza, movies, and kitty cuddles for as long as my cat Cheddar tolerated them before clawing his way to freedom.

This time, the goblin couldn't stop herself from rolling her eyes. "I am a warrior. I know just how much everything can hurt."

Touché. My training probably amounted to remedial kindergarten for a goblin warrior. "Yeah, well, I'm not used to it. Any chance we could reschedule this? I'm free all day tomorrow."

"The queen does not follow your schedule."

Realizing this was not something I could avoid, I used every ounce of willpower I possessed to stop myself from slamming my front door in the woman's face. "Okay, then can I have an hour to freshen up at least?"

She took in my coffee-stained jeans, ratty tennis shoes, and frizzy ponytail, and winced. "I am sorry, but we do not have time. We are already behind schedule."

I debated telling the lackey to inform the queen to shove it where the sun didn't shine, but I hadn't just spent six weeks and a couple grand trying to become a better Fortune for nothing. Telling the queen of another magical race to shove off would be stupid and likely make me a political pariah, possibly worse. Who knew what happened to people who pissed off Queen Delmy? It was in my best interests not to find out.

"Fine, but I'm not putting on the bag until I'm in the car. My neighbors already think I'm weird. And I need to get my purse and feed my cat. I'll be out in five."

Closing the door on the goblin before she could argue, I turned and went through the small foyer to the kitchen at the back of the house. I opened a can of tuna for my cat, while he weaved around my legs, purring.

"That's right, baby, mama missed you. You're gonna get tuna for a week." Once I plopped the tuna into his bowl, he immediately ignored me. Sighing, I grabbed my purse, checking to see that my phone and keys were safely tucked inside, before walking out. The nameless goblin sat in a black sedan with the engine running. I locked the deadbolt, quickly checked my wards, and approached the vehicle. When I climbed into the passenger seat she handed over the black hood wordlessly.

"Can you drive to the corner at least?"

She sighed and drove to the end of the street. I put on the hood without further comment.

Initially, I paid attention to which direction we were driving, but with my eyes covered, the smooth drive in the luxury sedan soon lulled me to sleep. I awoke when the car hit gravel, knocking my head against the window. Disoriented, I reached to pull off the hood.

"Don't take it off," the woman warned me.

My mind snapped into focus, and I relaxed a little in my seat as we jostled along. My mouth felt like cotton. I found a good reason to wear the hood. I may have been drooling in my sleep and the black fabric hid the evidence. The car came to a stop.

"Stay in your seat. I will come around to get you."

I heard her exit the vehicle and felt the cool December air hit me as she opened my door. Unsnapping the seat belt, I let her help me out. My feet met gravel, and I stumbled behind the goblin as she haphazardly dragged me along.

When I tripped over what felt like a large rock, I snapped. "I agreed to meet with your queen, not be led off a cliff."

The goblin woman snorted but didn't say anything. She came to a sudden stop, and I ran into her back before righting myself. She began to chant softly in a language I didn't understand, but my magic perked up and rushed forward to tickle my skin. The chanting stopped, and beneath my feet, the earth began to rumble. It probably should have freaked me out, but magic wasn't always subtle. After six weeks of intense magical training, my reaction was to yawn under my hood. Once again, the sucker came in handy since the goblin couldn't see my face under the fabric, so I didn't have to pretend to be impressed.

She grabbed my hand and dragged me forward once more. Soon the gravel path turned to what felt like smooth stone. Blindfolded, I started to focus on my other senses, namely my magic. A magic scan was somewhat rude, but the goblins' own magic wouldn't sense it, and after the forced wearing of the hood, I lacked my normal manners. There were roughly ten goblins in the general vicinity, but they were nowhere near me. Beyond them was the earth magic goblins possessed, blanketing the atmosphere. It was a magic I was intimately familiar with, thanks to a recently discovered, although unknown goblin ancestor somewhere back in my family line. In a happy accident, this heritage led to being gifted with my very own goblin plane, though my newly discovered bloodline and the whole owning of a plane thing wasn't common knowledge. The existence of goblin planes weren't common knowledge outside of the goblin community.

My musings ended when I ran into the woman's back yet again, and someone cleared their throat. The hood was yanked off, and I blinked a moment to clear my vision before I noticed the candlelit splendor before me. From the polished stone floor and stalactite shadows dancing in the dim light to the lavish Persian rugs and brocade-covered sofas, the cavern was a study in contradiction. The throne poised in the middle of it all completed the grandeur.

Artfully arranged metals were shaped into a wingback chair with burgundy leather cushions. It wasn't a stereotypical throne, but my skin tingled lightly at the waves of power radiating from it. Distracted by the chair, I failed to notice the approaching woman until the goblin who had driven me here stepped swiftly behind me.

Despite the room's splendor, I didn't know how I'd missed her presence. She was stunning. Long dark hair braided intricately hung in a rope over her shoulder. The eyes she shared with her son matched the deep-blue tunic she wore, which added an elegant touch to her dark pants and heeled boots. She was shorter than my five seven, but her presence made me feel like David to her Goliath. Unfortunately, I'd left my slingshot at home. I reached up to try to smooth my fly-aways, self-conscious of the wreck I must resemble.

She let me stare for a good thirty seconds before the corner of her mouth twitched. My mind told me that this would be a good time to introduce myself, but my tongue decided to stay glued to the roof of my mouth.

Finally, she inclined her head and put me out of my misery. "So, this is the little halfling that's been driving my son crazy and claiming her own plane in my domain." Her face remained stoic but the twitch at the corner of her mouth gave away her amusement.

"My family isn't sure about which relative it would be, so I think that halfling would be overstating it." My mouth and brain decided to reconnect and the words fell out.

She quirked a brow. "Do you think someone with such a low percentage would really be able to ensorcell a plane?"

"Really, it was George who ensorcelled me."

"George?"

Perhaps I should just impale myself on one of stalactites now? "It was weird to call it my plane, the plane, plane, so I named it...George."

She laughed then, deep and rich. "We do name our planes since they are sentient, but I've never heard of one named George." She looked behind me. "Let's keep that to ourselves, Griselda," she addressed the woman behind me.

Suddenly, I felt like kind of a dick for not asking the woman's name. To be fair, she'd come to my house ten minutes after I arrived home and basically demanded I consent to my own abduction. Staying on the conversational track, I asked, "Am I not supposed to tell people its name?"

"It's not usually discussed outside of close personal friends. I'm surprised Deval hasn't mentioned that to you."

Heat flooded my cheeks. The last time I'd seen her son Deval was right after we found the man who had stolen from him. That was the same time Deval implied he wanted to be more than friends. Shortly afterward, Pammy, sheriff of the Arizona witches and my boss, informed me about a last-minute training at a Fortune Boot Camp in Illinois. Because of the short notice, the organizers had lowered the price of the training from four grand to two. Despite the fact it wiped out quite a bit of my savings, it seemed like a good investment after my near-death experience on my last case, even if it meant missing Thanksgiving. "I haven't seen much of Deval recently, given that I've been out of town."

"Yes, I heard you've been away. I think my son has missed being called to your plane, I'm sorry, George."

"Uh, yeah, now that I'm back, I'm sure I'll invite him over," I muttered.

She arched a brow briefly before continuing. "Not a bad idea; however, that is not why I asked you here."

"Asked" was overstating things, but I bit my tongue. *My new training was already paying off.*

"I'm very glad you found the human thief," she continued. "Still, there is no way that a mortal male should have found the safe's original location unaided. He had to have had help, and I want you to find that help. Obviously, I will pay you."

My stomach twisted. Even with the new training, getting a job from the Queen of the Goblins was intimidating and frankly a bit out of my wheelhouse.

"It's not that I don't want to see that aspect through, Your Highness, but I have other obligations," I fibbed.

Her smile became brittle. I doubted she was ever told no. "Isn't a Soldier of Fortune, by definition, someone for hire?"

"Sure, in the classic definition, but in relation to witches, you know Pammy is the deciding factor in the jobs I take." I paused, then barreled forward: "I'm assuming you want me to take it because I'm an outsider with no strong ties to your community, but apparently I am one of you, at least in part."

"Deval said you were smart." She kept her face blank despite the compliment.

At that, my inner twelve-year-old preened. "Problem is, I don't want Pammy knowing about my heritage, some-thing even your son told me not to share. If I did, only more questions would come out of it. I don't want to be maimed or killed because I inadvertently told Pammy about the planes."

She waved her hand in the air. "Don't be silly. I've already spoken with Pammy, informing her that I want to hire you because of your knowledge of the human thief."

"Well, you should have led with that, but you're a fool if you think Pammy doesn't suspect that something else is going on." As soon as I said "fool," my stomach dropped, but it was too late.

If her eyes were freeze rays, I'd be a Peg Popsicle right about now. "I am many things Ms. Darrow, 'fool' is not one of them. I have no doubt that Pammy is well aware of some of our secrets, but I do not like making it easy for her. Besides, given your newfound heritage and inheritance, I would think you, too, would want to keep our secrets."

"I'm not against keeping your secrets, Your Highness, and I will, but I was a witch long before I knew I was part

7

goblin. At the end of the day, Pammy is my boss. More than that, she is our protector, and I wouldn't do anything I feel would betray her." Behind me, Griselda let out a grunt, and I tried to hide my wince. Maybe I'd said the wrong thing. Again.

The queen stared at me, bringing up her hand to tap her chin thoughtfully with an index finger. "I do appreciate honesty. As of right now, I don't believe there will be a conflict of interest. Besides, Pammy has already given her blessing to my hiring you. Are you interested in the job?"

Considering I'd just shelled out two grand, she already had Pammy's blessing, and my back was pretty much against I wall, I was interested. There went the dream of spending a couple of days of being a couch potato. "What's the pay?"

"If you find out how the safe was stolen within a week, I can pay five thousand."

"I'll do it," I said before my brain properly processed the offer. I was paid three thousand to catch a killer six weeks before, and that payout was only because the tentative connection to the vampires. The wheels in my brain turned slowly as I tried to convince myself that the imminent payday was because this woman was wealthy. It wasn't working. "I mean, why so much?" Peg Darrow, Master of Negotiation, not.

She smiled. "Second thoughts so soon?"

"Uh, yeah. Most of the time I do think before I speak, but when you throw out large numbers like that, my filter becomes a little lax."

She laughed softly. "I may have been guilty of that in my youth."

A snort sounded from Griselda.

Delmy's gaze swept to the goblin warrior, and the queen arched a brow. "Hmm?"

I turned to look at Griselda and was surprised to find the warrior bashfully staring at her feet. "Nothing, ma'am."

Not wanting to extend her discomfort, I turned my attention back to the queen. "Why are you willing to pay such a high price?"

"Are you asking what the catch is?"

"Are you actually going to tell me what it is?" I asked, my body stiff.

"Why not? Just do one thing for me first."

"Um, you're not asking me to murder anyone, right?"

She didn't miss a beat. "Not this time."

I swallowed.

She looked thoughtfully around the room before returning her gaze to me. "Please reach out with your magic and let me know if you sense anything. I have my own magics at work, but one can never be too careful."

That wasn't as bad as I thought it would be. "What exactly would you like me to scan for?"

"Any presence or magic that could be listening in."

Peg Darrow, witch counter-surveillance device. I called my magic to me. After the past six weeks of training, it had only grown stronger, and I was in my secret element. Goblins had innate magic, but they could build on their natural skills by pulling it from the earth and the precious metals and stones kept protected on their personal planes. Purely by accident, I'd learned my witch batteries got a big dose of energy from being on my plane and surrounded by stone. All of the benefits of goblin magic, with the added fluidity of witch magic. Deval and his mother weren't the only ones who wanted to keep my goblin heritage secret. Self-preservation was a wonderful motivator.

The magic flowed through me then reached out to caress the surrounding cavern before sinking past it, into the heart of the mountain. The same group of goblins I'd picked up on when I was first brought in were still out there, but well away from the chamber in which I stood. Not picking anything else up on the initial sweep, I turned my concentration to the room itself. It was warded, yes, but since I had the queen's permission, the wards kindly acquiesced to my explorative energy. Ten minutes later, I could say with confidence no one was listening besides Griselda, and I did.

Delmy's shoulders appeared to relax, but I couldn't be certain. "Good, one can never be too careful."

I nodded.

"What do you know of Prince Faxon?"

"He's your brother, right?"

"Yes, younger brother by about one hundred years. The moppet still thinks because he is male, he should be King."

"Sounds like an interesting family dynamic," I hedged.

Delmy gave me a thoughtful look. "See, you are capable of diplomacy. I thought so. He's an ass, but beyond being an ass, I believe he, or possibly one of his house, has traitorous intentions."

Oh dear gods. How did I keep getting these wonderful assignments? "Is that so?" I squeaked out.

"Very much so." She walked over to a freestanding bar, collected three rocks glasses, and then poured amber liquor into each. "Come here, Peg. You, too, Griselda. You've had a trying day."

I had to appreciate a woman who knew how to treat her staff, but really, Griselda had simply listened to me try to avoid this meeting for a few minutes, not headed negotiations with foreign dignitaries. I didn't roll my eyes though because I wanted whatever was in that glass. Normally, I considered myself a tequila kind of girl, but booze was booze. At Delmy's gesture, I walked forward and took the heavy-cut crystal glass.

Griselda came over, took a glass, and downed it, grunting her appreciation. As Griselda took her place again behind me, Delmy inclined her head. Instead of downing the liquid like Griselda had, I followed Delmy's lead and swirled the liquid in my glass before taking little sips, allowing the charred oaky flavor to coat my tongue.

A sip of liquid courage was all it took. I wanted this job for the money despite self-preservation sending a tinkling little alarm through my brain. I didn't want to think about those bells too hard.

"So, I find the ones responsible for helping Grant steal from your son. Let's say for the sake of argument, that it was your brother or one of his people who helped that human trash invade Deval's home. I'm not comfortable meting out any form of punishment. I may be part goblin, but I don't think it's appropriate and, forgive me if this is rude, but I'm not willing to be a potential patsy." My knees trembled but maybe the dim lighting would hide it. I continued to meet Queen Delmy's gaze.

That habit of a single brow rising that she and her son shared made another appearance. Meeting my gaze, she leaned back against the bar gracefully and took a healthy swallow before setting the glass down and pushing back off the bar to stand straight. "I do not need a patsy. I need proof. When you find the perpetrators, I would be very displeased if you were to confront them yourself. I need evidence from you, not justice."

She came forward and took my hand that was not holding my whiskey glass in a death grip. Staring into my eyes she continued, "I do not value you less because you are only part goblin. It has been long since I have had a halfling in my court, and I look forward to the mischief you will no doubt stir." With that, she dropped my hand abruptly, strode over to her throne, and sat, her arms draped over the arm rests, legs crossed, leaning into the chair. The air it gave it off was decidedly regal. "Give me your answer, Peg Darrow."

With that queenly demand, I slugged back what remained of my whiskey and said, "Yes," with more conviction than I felt. Guess we knew who the fool was.

2

The hood made a return appearance for the drive home. Again, I napped, drooling in my sleep. Feeling a little guilty, I handed Griselda the damp hood, but it really wasn't my problem. Kidnappers should launder their own hoods. It was just common courtesy.

I marched from the car up to my front door, but hesitated when I saw what waited for me. My stomach dropped. Sitting on the bench that adorned my porch was one of the loveliest arrangements of flowers I had ever seen. Two months ago, it would have been the hands-down winner. But in the process of catching a murderer and thief of goblin treasures, I'd come into direct contact with Fane Dimir, resident sociopathic vampire, and now my not-so-secret admirer.

Girding my loins, I walked up to the arranged flowers and picked them up. The large holiday arrangement was done admirably in greens, reds, and whites, with glittery ornaments protruding at tasteful increments. At least as tasteful as glitter could be. My sister referred to glitter as the bedbug of crafting. It showed up when one least expected it and was often hard to dispose of. Unlocking and then opening the door with one hand, I walked in and deposited the flowers on my small kitchen table.

Before I'd left for training in Illinois, there wouldn't have been a place to put them. My being Fane's object of affection meant new bouquets arrived every day, sometimes twice in the same day. Thanks to that schedule, I now knew that Marty, the flower guy, had three daughters and a son who was, in his opinion, a little "too good at arranging flowers" but hadn't come out yet. Marty thought I was one lucky lady to get so much attention. Because Marty was human, I didn't clue him in on the fact that in all actuality Fane wanted to torture, rape, and kill me because that was how he showed his affection. A shiver ran down my spine.

The flowers served as a reminder to keep training and get better at protecting myself, along with my friends and my family. Lola, my best friend who'd been house sitting for me while I was gone, had felt the best way to protect me was to throw the flowers away. Whether they stayed or not didn't bother me because the flowers, and Fane, were part of my current reality.

Pushing the blooms from my mind, I went back to the living room to begin the plans I'd had before being summoned. I had seven days to find the traitor, but nothing would get accomplished tonight. Delmy promised to send over a file tomorrow with all the relevant players, mainly Faxon and his sons. Tonight, I wanted to enjoy my freedom. A soda, a cat, and some TV were just what the doctor ordered. I even decided to go hog wild and order a pizza. Just when I was comfortably ensconced on the couch with Cheddar purring loudly on my legs, my phone blared a ring tone that I really didn't want to hear.

I used to like the song before. I mean there wasn't rest for anybody let alone the wicked, and money certainly didn't grow on trees. In what I thought was a brilliant move, I added it as a ringtone for my boss, the local witch sheriff. Now its only competition as the most hated sound my phone made was the tone used for my alarm. I did something I had never done in the short amount of time I had been a Fortune. I ignored the call. Not to say I sent the call to voice mail. Pammy was too smart to not to know what getting a voice mail after a couple of rings meant. I needed to be able to play dumb if she questioned me later.

When the song ended, I let out the breath I hadn't realized I'd been holding. Only to jump when the song began playing again immediately. Cheddar clawed me through the throw over my legs before climbing off. Damn it, there went my kitty love time. Sighing, I answered the phone. "Hello."

"Sug, why aren't you answering your phone?" Pammy did not sound happy.

"I was in the bathroom," I lied automatically.

"Hmmph." Yeah, Pammy wasn't buying it.

"Uh, yeah, sorry, what can I do for you?" I mumbled into the phone.

"You can get your ass down to the Christmas party. The McAllisters are in town, and one of them seems to be pretty cozy with your friend."

Huh? "Who are the McAllisters? And there's a Christmas party?"

"Girl, you need to check your email. Of course there's a Christmas party, or Hanukkah, Winter Solstice, Krampus, or get-drunk-on-Pammy's-dime party. Whatever floats your boat; I myself like Jesus better than I like Krampus, so I've made my choice."

Glad to know my workplace wasn't discriminatory. Of course, since everyone else discriminated against witches, we tried to be pretty open in our own community. "Sounds like a good time, but I have had a long day. Besides, I don't know the McAllisters, so it would be weird to stop by and say 'hi,' even if they know one of my friends."

"Do you think I would drag you in for this if it wasn't important? Do I need to call in your token?"

"Seriously?" I asked, incredulous. Tokens were part of the Soldier of Fortune contract. Every job we did was paid by the client. If the client couldn't pay, but the matter needed to be addressed, the Benefactor would spot the bill. We were our own nation and policed our own through the mercenary system. A caveat of signing on as one of those mercenaries was that we agreed to grant the local sheriff one token job a year.

"You bet your ass I am."

"I thought the sheriffs rarely collected tokens. Not to mention I've only been working for you for like three months!"

"Well, I only collect them when I need them, and these slimy motherfuckers have come to my town, and you've already got an in. Right now I need that in. Come down here, and I won't make you the principal investigator."

I sat forward, swinging my legs off so my feet rested on the floor, I pinched the bridge of my nose. With my new job I didn't have time to take on another investigation. "Who exactly is my 'in'?"

"Lola."

My heart began to race. Sure, I didn't know who, or what, the McAllisters were, but if they bothered Pammy, I sure as hell didn't want them anywhere near my best friend. "I'll be there in fifteen." I stood up. "Wait, where is the party?"

Pammy grunted into the phone. "No, you will not. You will be here in an hour and fifteen. It's a holiday party, not a pajama party, and I want you to look festive. It's at my usual location."

"You're holding your Christmas party at Bump and Grind?" I asked, referring to the local strip mall coffee shop at which Pammy held court.

"Course I am, but it's catered, and we've set up a bar."

She should have started with the three magic words "coffee, food, and booze." If she had, there would be no need to threaten me with the token card. "I thought this was an emergency?"

"It's not an emergency, it's a situation, and one I want your assistance with. Now, go put on some lipstick and come to the party." Pammy hung up on me.

Closer to an hour and a half later, I walked into the independent coffee bar in Tempe. Per Pammy's request, I was suitably done up in a red sweater dress, with heeled boots. I pulled out all the stops, including some winged eyeliner, and the requisite red lipstick. The heels were already starting to hurt, but I didn't think there was going to be a rumble tonight, and I rarely dressed up, so I thought it would be safe to wear them.

Scanning the room, I was glad I had taken Pammy's demand seriously. There was quite a crowd, but one guest in particular caught my eye. Deval, the goblin prince, stood in the center of the room in a three-piece charcoal suit, looking quite handsome. My feet started to move of their own accord until a stunning raven-haired goblin glided to his side and wrapped her arm around his waist. My spine stiffened, and I stopped short. Deval reached to place his arm around his date when his eyes suddenly snapped to meet mine. Surprise sparked in his gaze, and his hand seemed to hesitate on her shoulder.

He's not my boyfriend, I reminded myself. Not wanting to see, I turned away and shook my head. We had a hint of a connection, but I wouldn't throw myself at someone who wanted someone else.

Lola, my best friend, appeared at my side. "I hate her."

The rock forming in the pit of my stomach dissolved instantly as I bent over laughing.

"I'm serious, Peg. She's a total snob. She used to date one of my foster brothers."

Lola always hated her brothers' girlfriends, but I knew better than to mention that. "Oh really, which one?"

"Arick, he always goes for high maintenance."

I took in Lola's perfectly arranged blonde hair, artful makeup, and silvery cocktail dress with shoes to match and arched a brow.

Her lips pursed. "Don't look at me like that. I look good in khakis and work boots, too. Besides, I'm just as likely to shop at Target as at Nordstrom's, and I don't insist on diamonds as gifts from boys I've been seeing for two weeks."

"She really did that?" My face scrunched up.

"Gold. Digger." Lola pronounced, clipping each word.

"Oh now, love, I would never call you that." Suddenly a handsome man was at Lola's elbow.

She giggled, batting away his hand. "Peg, this is Michael McAllister." She smiled up at the man with a look of adoration that usually went the other way.

I studied the tall, thin man with the wheat-colored hair a few shades darker than Lola's. He was handsome, but the smile he bestowed on Lola didn't reach his eyes. My stomach tightened with dread. I forced a smile to my lips and held out a hand. He grasped it in a bone crushingly firm handshake. Taken aback, I sent a little shock through my palm. Most other witches would have pulled back, but he gave me a pleased smile. It was creepy.

"Lola said you attended a Fortune Boot Camp recently. It appears to have gone well for you."

My brow furrowed. Other witches didn't usually comment on another's power level. "Uh, thank you. How do you two know each other?"

He let go of my hand, draping his arm across Lola's shoulders. "This angel and I knew each other as children. When my family came back to Arizona, I had to look her up." He gave Lola another false smile. Her returning grin made it apparent that she didn't see the act.

"Isn't it great, Peg? Michael was my first love." She mooned at him.

I worked to keep my face neutral. "I don't remember him."

He let out a laugh tinged with scorn. "Of course not. Lola and I knew each other before she moved to Phoenix." Lola was originally from Tucson but had moved to Phoenix to live with her father's best friend and his family, goblins, after her parents' death.

"Oh, so you're from Tucson then?" I prodded.

"No, my family are a traveling people. We don't like to stay in one place too long." He looked at his watch. "Speaking of which, look at the time. Lola, we promised my mother we would stop by for a visit tonight."

Lola pouted. "But Peg just got here, and I haven't seen her for six weeks."

"You said you would visit. It would be very rude of you to keep my mother waiting." His voice hardened.

My face heated at his tone, and I waited for Lola to rip him a new one.

She blinked once but then smiled sweetly. "Of course,

you're right, Michael. That was thoughtless of me." Turning to me, she kissed my cheek and enveloped me in a hug. "Can't wait to catch up." Just like that, she was whisked away into the night.

My mouth was still hanging open in shock when Pammy barreled up to me. "See what I mean, Sug?"

I managed to close my mouth after making a few guppy-like faces. I raised my hand, pointing at the door. "What the hell just happened?"

"You tell me. It may be a party, but we have work to do."

I dropped my hand and thought for a moment. "Is something wrong with Lola?"

Pammy shook her head. "McAllisters are bad news. Reports of missing witches happen whenever they're in town, but I scanned her to make sure she wasn't under any spell that I could find without being invasive. There may be something, but there's also plain old infatuation and stupidity at work."

I swung back to face Pammy. "What the hell, Pammy? If they have that reputation, why would you let Lola leave with them?" My voice bordered on a shout. The volume of the party lulled as one song ended and another began. When I looked up from Pammy's angry gaze, I found all eyes were on us, including Deval's. He arched a brow at me that twenty minutes ago I would have found attractive, but now I wanted to punch his smug face. Before I could follow that train of thought, Pammy's strong fingers dug in to my arm.

"You did not just speak to me like that," she muttered, dragging me out the front door. A few people stood outside, sneaking drunken cigarettes. Pammy gave them a look, and they scattered, dropping the butts on the ground. Spectators gone, she turned the look on me.

I balked a little, wanting to run, too. "Okay, I shouldn't have raised my voice in public, but how would you have felt if I told you that someone had a reputation for making witches disappear after your best friend had just left with him?" With a lot of willpower, I managed to keep my voice calm and steady.

Pammy folded her arms over her broad chest. "Peg, do I take care of my own?"

My first thought was *as long as they don't oppose you,* but then I really thought about it. Pammy did things I didn't like, and she wasn't the kindest to her opposition, but she wouldn't stand aside while another witch was going to be hurt unless it was sanctioned.

"Yes," I ground out.

"If the McAllisters are who I believe in my gut they are, they're elusive. We need an in. Lola is our in. They won't harm her when they publicly left with her. They're careful. What did you feel when you shook his hand?"

"My bones being crushed," I answered wryly.

"Yeah, he pulled that shit on me. So, I did it right back to him."

"I zapped him." My face heated a little.

Pammy tsked, shaking her head. "Bad form, Sug, but beyond etiquette, don't give him a taste of your power."

I frowned. "What do you mean give him a taste?"

"They're rumored to be Drainers."

A moment ago I felt heated, now I felt cold at the mere mention of the word. "Why are they still alive?"

"Can't prove it."

"That's not good enough. If they're even suspected, why are they allowed to stay here?"

Pammy was quiet for a moment. "You would want me to shove them off on some other city? Where maybe people didn't suspect what they were?"

I pinched the bridge of my nose and closed my eyes for a moment. "No, so what are you going to do?"

"We're gonna be smart." She emphasized the 'we.' "Lola is our in."

"Does she know?"

"Nope, and she wouldn't listen anyway. She's under his spell."

"As in a literal spell?"

"I already told you, I don't think so, but with that level of infatuation, she may as well be. We can't go in guns blazing. We need to be careful. The McAllisters have been around for a long time. I first heard about them thirty years ago. They pop up in a place, and then they go underground for a while before too many questions can be asked. We need to snag them before they move on, got it?"

"How long do they usually stay in a place?" I asked.

"Couple of weeks. Sometimes they only pop up for a week. They usually send someone ahead of time to blend in and get the lay of the land."

I nodded. "Michael mentioned his mother was here. He insisted that Lola leave with him to go visit her."

"Mmhmmm, I'd bet good money that woman isn't using the McAllister name. I'd like to invite her for coffee, if you'd care to pass the message through Lola. I know you've got a gig with the goblins, but remember, Peg, you're a witch first. I'm not saying to offend Delmy, but if humans knew someone was draining people, it would drag up history from four hundred years ago. We don't need another witch trial."

I hadn't even thought of that. My eye began to twitch. "How have they not been caught?"

"Humans don't like us very much, Sug, as you well know, and the McAllisters only drain witches."

"Just peachy," I muttered.

3

A hard knock reverberated through my house at seven on the dot. Griselda stood on my doorstep, looking cheerful. At least as cheerful as someone who didn't smile could look.

"Good morning, Griselda, before I offer you coffee just promise me you don't have a black bag on you?"

The corners around her mouth pinched. "Of course not. I'm just bringing by the file that the queen promised."

"Well, come on in." I opened the door wider.

She shoved a leather-bound binder at me. "That won't be necessary."

I fumbled to grab the binder as she turned swiftly on her heel, marching to her black sedan without a farewell. Snorting, I closed my door and walked back to the kitchen where the coffee was conveniently located. *Coffee that I didn't have to share with anyone.* I set the binder on the table and poured myself a large mug along with some pumpkin creamer. If that was basic, I didn't want to be complicated. Sleep had eluded me the night before. Not wanting to make small talk with Deval and his date, I'd left the party directly after my tête-à-tête with Pammy.

Taking my coffee to the table, I unzipped the deceptively hefty leather binder. The only thing I found inside was a very thin manila folder containing about ten pages in total. I flipped through them, staring at them incredulously; suddenly wishing I could rewind twenty-four hours and turn Delmy down. She hadn't said it would be easy, but I didn't have time to play super sleuth now that Lola was in danger. Taking a deep breath, I remembered that Pammy had said we had some time and looked more closely at the pages that had been provided.

They were surveillance notes from a PI. If Delmy had a Private Investigator, why did she need me? Then, I realized that whoever took these notes likely hadn't retired down to Tucson. Goblins were good at hiding bodies, earth magic, and all that. I swallowed and began a thorough read through. The majority of the surveillance had been on Gregar and Vegard, Faxon's two sons. I had met them a couple of months ago when I had been investigating the theft of the goblin safe.

Vegard had been pretty nice in the few moments I'd spoken to him. Gregar, on the other hand, had been a total tool. Both brothers appeared to frequent nightclubs, but different ones. According to the sparse notes done by the PI, the brothers didn't get along. The investigator believed that Gregar followed his father's mindset and believed Faxon was heir to the throne. Vegard didn't seem to care, which angered Gregar.

When I saw the places that they liked to frequent, it was pretty clear which brother I would target first in my investigation. Gregar's hangouts of choice were boys' club cigar bars and strip clubs. Since I didn't have dollar bills to throw around and was no aficionado of cigars, I decided to hit up Vegard's hangout, The Ranch. The place was an upscale roadhouse. An oxymoron, I knew. It had a huge indoor space with a large dance floor, plus the place took advantage of the Arizona weather and offered a large outdoor area complete with bonfires. The place was known for its craft beer. If I attempted to order domestic beer there, I would be shunned.

I yawned and took another sip of my coffee. I considered a nap but remembered that I had something even better than coffee to give me a boost in my step. It felt sacrilegious to even think it, but it was true. I set my empty mug in my sink and went to grab the winter parka I had purchased while in Illinois and slid my feet into some slippers. In the living room, I eyed George, my artful metal chest slash secret goblin plane, with awe. I ran my fingers over the gold and bronze and silver scroll work. The chest seemed to vibrate in appreciation at my attention. I opened the lid and took the stone steps that only I could see down into the chilly desert landscape that was all mine.

I found my sleeping stone, which was more of an almost accidental death stone because I had fallen asleep on it before when I hadn't been used to George's magic, and I had nearly died. Shrugging, I sat cross-legged on it and pretended to meditate, all the while feeling my magic get topped off and my energy levels soar. It was an energy drink without a crash. Goblins could pull magic from their planes from a distance. My strange surprise heritage didn't allow that to my knowledge, but it was way better than having to sleep for a day and eat a steak to recharge…well, maybe.

Properly restored, I headed back upstairs to shower and wash my hair. An early start was necessary, and I needed to get the time-consuming process of blow-drying my hair finished. After a much-too-rushed shower, the laborious activity began. Head down, ass up in the bathroom, I heard a muffled noise. Straightening, I turned off the blow dryer and realized someone was knocking on my door. Since Griselda had already brought over the file, I wasn't expecting anyone. I walked to the front door. Cheddar, decided to rise from whatever nook he had been napping in and come with me to investigate. Three feet from the door, he went all Halloween cat on me, tail up, fur bristled, spitting at the door before taking off to return to one of his hiding spots. The hair on the back of my neck to stood up.

Only one person—*monster*, I corrected—would cause that reaction. Fane Dimir. Head of the local vampire clan and my personal stalker. Taking a breath, I reached out with my magic, making sure my wards were held strong. They were.

I considered not answering at all, and then Fane's voice cut through my front door.

"Peg, I know you're home. Don't you want to see me?" His voice had an almost childlike earnestness to its tone. He was trying to appear harmless when he was anything but. I didn't want to open the door, but it wasn't smart to run and hide from predators. It only piqued their interest.

I opened the door. "Fane, what an unpleasant surprise." I made a special effort to avoid eye contact with him. Witches had lost their immunity to vampire glamour when they lost their immortality to a curse during the witch trials.

He smiled, showing off his second set of canines that while sheathed, looked just a little sharper than average and made for a toothy grin. "Come now, Peg, you know you missed me. I know I missed you when you went out of town and didn't tell me. What a naughty little bunny you are." In the past when I had spoken with him, he'd appeared a little less insane. Maybe a vampire's way to show affection was to let all the crazy out. Not, looking through someone's phone crazy but straight up psychotic stalker crazy. *Yep, that makes sense.*

"Fane, I liked the flowers, but I'm never going to be your plaything. This infatuation will lead nowhere. I'm not my aunt, and I have no desire to be anyone's blood slave. I work for Pammy, who wouldn't let me be taken without coming after me. I'm friendly with the goblins as well. Do you really want to start an incident?"

Fane held up a hand and waggled a finger at me. "Don't be silly, pet. You'll love it when you come with me, well, until you don't love it, but I'll love the part that you don't love, so we'll both be happy."

"Let me guess, the part I won't love is torture?" I crossed my arms and gave a hard stare at the bridge of his nose, avoiding eye contact, pretty much the most aggressive look I could give with our curse in place.

He chuckled. When Fane laughed, all of the pretenses of being human melted away and some primitive part of my brain told me to run. I clenched the doorknob more tightly, glad that my hand was hidden from view behind the door.

"I really like you, Peg. I wish we could start our courtship now, but I came to tell you that I have matters I must attend to. Namely, I told Alice that I knew what she is, and then she had the audacity to leave town."

"What?" My eyebrows drew together.

"Oh good, you didn't know. I don't like it when my toys talk to one another too much. It gives them ideas."

The fear momentarily fled as my hand not holding the doorknob flexed into a fist. I was nobody's fucking toy. "I could say this has been a pleasure, Fane, but it hasn't. I hope you have a lovely trip, drive off a cliff, and are decapitated in the process." I ended on a smile.

"Bunny, you say such lovely things. Though I may need to punish you later. I may be gone a week or two. Stay out of trouble." He reached out as though to pat me on the head, but the wards stopped his hand midair. He frowned, "We'll need to do something about those." With that he turned and strode down to a waiting SUV. Looking over, I saw that he didn't have another vampire with him. Unsurprising, given how territorial vampires were. It was a miracle that they had managed to form any government at all.

The burst of adrenaline that had rushed my body at the interaction with Fane faded just as quickly leaving me nauseated and shaky. I hadn't realized that Alice was out of town. After our standoff with Grant, the cursed human that had stolen Deval's safe, Fane had told Alice that he had known what she was, but I had no idea what that meant. To me she was simply a scholar, and my teacher, slightly nutty, but in an endearing way. After closing my door and locking it, I grabbed my phone, calling Pammy. She answered on the third ring.

"Whatcha got for me?"

I sat on my couch, my legs still feeling wobbly. Cheddar came out of his hiding spot to head-butt me reassuringly. "Actually, I hoped that you would have something for me," I said while I reached over to scratch Cheddar's head.

"Hmmm, what's that?"

"Fane stopped by."

There was a long pause on the phone before Pammy responded. "When it rains, it fucking pours. I hoped that his obsession with you would be fleeting."

"Apparently not," I responded.

"Well, what are you asking for? A good old-fashioned

vampire hunt? I'm not going to lie to you, sweet cheeks, I don't think the Arizona witches are prepared for a war right this minute."

So reassuring. "I don't need to worry for a week or two. He's hunting someone else at the moment. He just came over to tell his 'pet' that he would be out of town for a week or two and to behave in his absence." I cringed.

There was a pause. "Well, that is not good."

"Yep, but I already knew this would be an issue. I'm more worried about Alice right now. She's the one who's on his radar."

"Alice isn't even in town right now," Pammy paused. "Ah shit, he's chasing after her now, too?"

"Yup, Fane has decided to seek her out, and I don't think it's to ask her to research ancient vampire lore."

"Alice is a powerful witch, and I'm sure that her blood would give Fane quite the boost, but she is well loved and connected. What aren't you telling me?" Pammy's deep voice took on a rough edge.

I hesitated only a second before I spilled the beans. "When we were trapped by Grant, and Fane came and killed him, Fane told Alice that he knew what she was. I'm not sure what he meant, but when he said it, he sounded like he coveted whatever that was. I'm not sure if he wants to cage her or kill her."

"Could be a million and four different things. Vampires like to collect, people, things, powers, whatever. Alice got a disposable cell. I'll give her a call and tell her to be on the lookout."

My hand relaxed on the throw pillow I hadn't realized I'd been clenching. "Thank you."

"No thanks needed, Sug. Alice and I have been friends for decades. I don't want anything happening to her either. Also, despite my dire pronouncement about not being ready for war, don't think that I won't fight for you. What kind of sheriff would I be if I didn't take care of my own?"

"Thank you, Pammy. That's very reassuring."

We hung up, and I sat in my living room in the quiet. I wasn't reassured in reality. Trouble had been marking me for a while, but I pushed at the ever darkening clouds, trying to focus on the here and now and not the possible gruesome eventualities that currently haunted my mind.

So, lost in my own melancholy, I jerked off of the couch when a knock sounded on my door yet again. My racing heart slowed the minute I heard Lola's cheerful voice.

"Open up, Peg. I brought Bosa's." She referred to a popular, local doughnut chain.

I opened the door. "Woman, don't you have a key?"

"Yep, but hell if I know where it is."

Great, just what I needed.

She scooted past me, taking the cardboard box to the kitchen. "Have you started coffee yet?"

"Of course I have, but the pot's empty. I didn't expect to see you this morning." Despite the surprise visit, seeing Lola alone, as her normal self, safe in my kitchen, eased a weight of worry off my chest.

Setting the box and her purse on my small kitchen table, she went about making another pot of coffee. "Of course, I'm going to come see you today! I've missed you. I have so much to tell you."

"I missed you, too," I said, sitting down at the table and opening the box. Eleven donuts sat before me. "I see that you got hungry on your way over." I laughed.

Lola looked up from measuring out the grounds a mischievous grin on her face. "If you can resist the smell, then you're not a person I want to associate with."

I nodded in agreement, taking a simple glazed donut

from the box. I enjoyed variety in my baked goods, but sometimes simplicity won. The light fluffy texture hit my tongue, and my eyes practically rolled back in appreciation.

Lola finished her task and came over and sat opposite me. "I know we talked on the phone, but tell me about your training."

I took her hand impulsively and sent a wave of power out. Her eyes widened. "Is that the training or your plane?"

"Both." I'd always been blessed with a large amount of magic, but between George, the magical plain, and my new control, it was stronger and better trained.

"That is impressive, babe. I wish I could do that, but it would probably just tickle you." She made a face.

"Wanna sign up for Fortune Boot Camp?"

She laughed, shaking her head. "I'll stick with being a mining engineer. I have enough power."

I nodded in agreement. Lola truthfully was not at my level and wouldn't be without some serious sacrifices, but she had a good level and was no weakling.

"Any interesting Fortunes at this training?" She waggled her eyebrows.

"There were some interesting people," I hedged.

"Mmmhmm, but you were thinking about Deval the whole time, weren't you?"

My skin heated. "Nope, after last night I've decided that's off limits. We can be friends, but I really don't want to be just another conquest. My novelty would wear off. Plus there's the fact that I will age, and he won't. I talked to Bruce about this before. It doesn't end well." I brought up our mutual shifter friend. The problem with being the only supernatural community with a normal human life expectancy was that it put us on an uneven playing field with people that should be our equals.

Lola stood, returned to the coffee maker, and poured out two mugs, doctoring them to our specifications before bringing them back to the table. Setting my cup in front of me, she gave me a thoughtful look. "I don't think you two can be just friends. There's something there, and I would suggest exploring where it could go."

I took a sip of the coffee before responding. "There is, but if it's something strong, then he should have been able to last six weeks out of my presence."

Lola rolled her eyes. "You two are not exclusive."

"I know that." I started, but Lola held up her hand.

"Real life is not a romance novel. Relationships take time, and you can't expect everyone to be on the same timeline as you. You didn't even tell him you were leaving."

"Hey, I sent him an email. It was very last minute." I said feeling defensive.

Lola let out a deep sigh. "Peg, I'd bet these doughnuts that he took that as a brush off. He may have attended the party with what's-her-nuts, but once you got there, he couldn't stop looking over at you."

"How would you know? You left with Michael the minute he said jump." I regretted the words as soon as they left my mouth. I did not want to start this conversation like this.

Lola sat back abruptly. "What's that supposed to mean?"

"It means nothing," I lied. "I've just never seen you leave me so quickly for a man who you were dating." I tried to smooth it over, but her eyes remained sharp.

"This is about you feeling abandoned?" Her tone sounded harsh.

I shook my head. "This is coming out wrong. I want you to ditch me for Mr. Right, but he seemed really domineering. I didn't like the way he spoke with you. There are rumors—."

"There are always rumors when a new witch comes to town. I didn't think that you would be the type to join in the gossip. For the record, I've known Michael longer than I've known you."

"Yes, you mentioned knowing him as a child, but where has he been? Why have I never heard about him before, if you have such a strong relationship with this guy?"

"Peg, I don't share every little nuance of my life with you. I don't like talking about before…." She stopped, swallowing.

I saw it then, the unshed tears that shimmered in her eyes. Anger and sadness warred on her face. She was remembering the time before her parents died.

"Lola," I reached my hand out to her.

She recoiled from me. "Don't."

I pulled my hand back and looked down.

"I'm going to go now. When you're ready to be supportive, then feel free to give me a call." Lola snatched her purse and the doughnut box and left, slamming the front door.

I picked up the half eaten donut from before and took a bite. It suddenly tasted too sweet. The fault lay on the emotions rumbling through my brain and less on the quality of the donut. Sighing, I stood placing the half-eaten donut in the trash.

The argument with Lola could not have come at a worse time. I needed her to stay close to me, so I could watch her until we took care of her new boyfriend. *Great, now I sound like I've joined the mob*. Pammy might be amused if I referred to her as the godfather. She wouldn't want to be called the godmother, since that brought the fairy godmother connotations, and fae we were not.

Lola had always been willing to stew for days, leaving me in a purgatory, when we got into fights, whereas I preferred to hash things out immediately. I called her. She didn't answer, so I left a message apologizing. Five minutes later, I still gripped my phone willing a response. I sent her a text again apologizing and inviting her to go on a super secret mission to The Ranch that evening to talk to Vegard. Lola couldn't resist a good night out. Add a little bit of intrigue, and she really couldn't. I got a response two minutes later

Fine. I'll meet you there at eight.

Still mad at me obviously, but I'd take it.

4

Walking into The Ranch, I wished that Lola had ridden with me. She was a lot more familiar with the Scottsdale scene. After I valeted my bright-turquoise vintage Jeep Grand Cherokee, I stood awkwardly in front of the club. I looked down at the dress and fancy cowboy boots I'd donned to "fit in" at the bar, biting my lip.

"You look perfect."

I glanced up and saw Lola that had donned a similar outfit and sighed in relief.

She gave me a shy smile. "I think I may have overreacted earlier."

"I shouldn't have said that. It wasn't what I meant." I tried to explain.

"I know," she cut me off. "We can talk about that later. Now what was this super secret goblin mission you promised me?"

Briefly I explained that I just wanted to get a feel for Vegard. She nodded and led me into the club. She spotted our prey within one minute of walking in to the huge, open floor plan of the bar, pointing to a reserved table that was half in the building half in their outdoor space with its own fire pit.

"There he is."

"Damn, Lola, do you have goblin royalty radar?"

She laughed. "I'd have thought you did after you immediately spotted Deval at Pammy's holiday get together."

"Shut up," I muttered.

It only made her laugh harder. "Silly goose, I did a magic scan of the VIP areas. I can't blame you, by the way. If I hadn't grown up around him, Deval would be on my radar." She was trying to break the tension from our earlier fight.

"What do you mean?" I raised my voice a level as the DJ pumped up the music.

"Peg, he's always been an adult to me. Meaning, he's like a favorite uncle. The hot uncle, but still the uncle. No. Interest." She emphasized.

"It's for the best. He's trouble."

"They usually are. I'm so glad I found Michael."

I almost gagged at the sharp reminder of the man. "That's nice, Lola," I choked out.

"Shall we?" She motioned to Vegard, who was surrounded by a bevy of human beauties.

Personally, I was intimidated by the velvet ropes and the burly security guard who looked like he said things like "Let's crack skulls." Lola, though, had a lot more experience with this kind of thing and apparently knew the skull cracker.

"Terrance!" she squealed, putting a little more jiggle in her step.

"Hey, Lo, what's going on, girl?" Terrance didn't smile, likely because that would ruin his image, but his eyes did light up a little.

"Oh, you know, just work, the usual. How are your daughters?"

That got a hint of a twitch at the corner of his mouth. "Beautiful little terrors. My wife keeps calling them Terrance's Terrors."

"I bet." Lola grinned, genuinely happy to hear about this man's daughters, so her next question didn't feel as manipulative as it should have. "Terrance, I need to talk to a gentleman in there. Any chance you can let a couple of ladies in?"

He didn't even raise a brow. "As it happens, the gentleman paying for this table said to feel free to invite any fine young things. You and your friend definitely meet the requirements." He looked me up and down without ogling. Quite the feat. He opened the rope, gesturing us in.

I thanked him as we passed. Lola immediately approached the table and reached out her hand to the gentleman currently draped in the "fine young things" that Terrance had described.

"I'm Lola," she said, hitting him with a megawatt smile.

He fumbled a little to untangle himself from his current cohorts, standing to clasp her hand in both of his like a gentleman. He leaned in, and I heard him whisper to Lola. "A pleasure to meet you. Tell me, Lola, are we family?"

That was supernatural speak for who or what are you.

She nodded. "I'm the adopted daughter of Amery and Amalda Degroot. You've likely seen me around."

"And, I've never introduced myself? How amiss of me. And you have Ms. Darrow with you. How nice." He turned meeting my eyes. So much for staying on the down low.

37

I gave him a rueful grin. "I'm surprised that you recognized me."

"I never forget a beautiful woman."

"And yet you didn't remember, Lola?"

He flashed me a grin, "I knew I'd seen her before. Perhaps I was too shy to introduce myself."

Lola's dimples made an appearance, and she playfully batted him on the arm. "You tease, too bad you're too late now."

He covered his heart with his hand. "Say it isn't so, fair maiden."

"Meh, it's new; give it a week." I piped in.

Lola's head snapped back, and she gave me a dark look. Before I could so much as shrug, she turned back to Vegard.

He had thrown up his hands. "Ladies, I didn't mean to cause a tiff."

Lola stayed silent, so I took over. "Pssssh, we've been friends for years. It takes a lot more than an off comment to get us into a tiff."

Lola gave me a look that suggested that wouldn't be the case later but plastered a smile back on her face.

I shrugged.

"I need a drink," she mumbled before sitting on the loveseat.

Vegard had to be confused at the strange interaction, but he didn't miss a beat. He snapped his fingers and a waitress, scantily clad in a vest and chaps with boy shorts underneath, appeared, eager to earn an extra tip on top of whatever ridiculous amount was added as gratuity on the overpriced bottle service.

A moment later, both Lola and I had vodka sodas in our hands, mine with a lemon, and hers with a lime. I took a seat next to Lola and gave her knee a friendly squeeze before Vegard took a seat next to her. The women who had previously held Vegard's attention looked slightly annoyed, but since they still had access to bottle service, we were only a mild irritation.

"So," Vegard said, taking a sip of a smoky-looking liquor in a rocks glass, "How did I get so lucky to get the honor of two beautiful witches' attention tonight."

Lola didn't miss a beat, "Oh, we were just out, and I saw you and decided we should finally meet. After all, you'd already met Peg."

He glanced at me smiling. "Yes, we did. My cousin wanted to shoo her off, and my brother likely wanted to murder her."

I arched a brow. "Murder me?"

"He is a difficult man." He shrugged, indicating that his brother's desire for my imminent death was no big deal.

I swallowed. "I hope you don't share his sentiment," I forced out.

He looked surprised. "Of course not. I don't have problems with anyone."

"Not even your cousin?" I asked skeptically. "You and your brother seemed...challenging toward him when I last saw you."

Lola leaned back into the cushions, letting our conversation fly over her.

He laughed. It wasn't a friendly laugh. "Do not confuse me with my brother."

I was about to reply when suddenly Michael was at the rope, giving Lola a look that should be reserved for serial killers and puppy abusers.

Lola saw him as well, hopping up. "Hope you don't mind, Peg, I invited Michael."

She didn't leave me time to respond before sauntering over to get Michael admitted to the VIP area. I studied them from afar. Michael's stiff body language seemed to radiate anger. He didn't come in the ropes but had Lola come out to him, giving her a kiss on the cheek.

Lola turned around, calling out to us. "Ladies' room, be back in a few."

Michael frowned at her but escorted her away. Part of me wanted to follow to make sure she'd be fine, but I needed to talk to Vegard, and we were in a public place. Before I could turn back to Vegard, Michael was back at the rope alone. He didn't appear to be trying to get into the area. I saw a subtle flick of his wrist aimed at Vegard before he turned, walking quickly away.

I shot out my arm, comprehension flashing through my mind. My power surged forward, trying to block whatever Michael had thrown at Vegard.

The magic shredded my defensive spell. Michael's power seemed to treat my own shield as a colander. I'd limited the damage, but bits and pieces of his magic made it through and hit Vegard. A few stray tendrils hit me as well, feeling like hot needles in my arm and making it difficult to fill my lungs completely. I looked down. Vegard's goblin skin usually had a slightly ashy undertone, but now he was positively gray, and the shallow up and down of his chest suggested his breathing was also restricted. I glanced up, concerned with having to protect Vegard, but Michael had disappeared into the crowd.

The women in the VIP area started to gather around Vegard's prone form in concern. I shooed them back, saying I was a paramedic. I opened his shirt and saw the angry welts that came from dirty magic, but no one else was the wiser, so it was accepted when I said there had been an allergic reaction. Hovering over his body, I placed my hand over his heart. Reaching out with my power, I felt the spell restricting it and his lungs. I sent some of my power into him, but it was just a Band-Aid on a bullet wound. Vegard took a strangled breath and sat up in pain.

I got close and whispered in his ear. "You've been hit by a nasty spell. I need to get you out of here, so I can call your cousin and go someplace where I can heal you away from humans."

His eyes were clouded, but he nodded in agreement. Thank the gods. I considered casting a spell to lessen his weight, but I couldn't drain my powers right now; I needed them to heal him and possibly defend us, so I called Terrance over.

He looked at us, realized that a VIP was down, and rushed to Vegard. "What's going on?"

"Allergic reaction," Vegard and I said at the same time.

Terrance gave us the once over with a grim look. I couldn't read minds, but it was obvious he was thinking drug use. "I'll call 911." He reached for his earpiece.

"No, I have an EpiPen in my car. I need help getting him there."

Terrance gave us an incredulous look, but at the nod from Vegard, he helped him stand up. I took one side, Terrance took the other, and we helped Vegard stagger out of the club. The two minutes it took the valet to retrieve my car were possibly the longest two minutes of my life. Vegard had started to sweat profusely, and I knew he wouldn't stay conscious much longer. It took a lot to kill a goblin; their natural life spans normally around a thousand years, but I didn't know what Michael had thrown at Vegard. The Jeep pulled up, and I threw cash at the attendee while Terrance loaded Vegard in and closed the door while I raced around to the other side and climbed in. My hands were shaking as I inserted the key and turned. Pulling out, I called Deval.

A few months ago, I had been the injured party and

had been taken to Deval's public condo. He also had a secret lair somewhere, but I had no idea where. I began to drive in the general direction of the condo, not quite sure of the exact location. Deval didn't answer. I hung up and immediately hit the re-dial button.

Vegard moaned in the backseat. Phone to my ear, I looked over at him. Could his skin get any grayer?

"Damn it, answer your phone," I muttered into the still ringing phone.

Deval must have just answered because I received the sunny response. "Perhaps I should hang up. You're already cursing at me. Is this about Patrice?"

"What?" I asked, confused before remembering his date at the Christmas party. "No, you moron. Your cousin Vegard has been hit with a dirty spell. I need to know exactly where to take him. I'm currently driving toward the area of your condo, but I can go elsewhere. Also, I need your healer to meet me, if possible. This magic needs to be pulled from him pronto, and I need to remove some from myself. And for the record, I don't give a damn who you're fucking."

5

Deval rattled off directions without further preamble, understanding the severity of the situation. I drove like someone was dying because Vegard didn't look so good and the traces of Michael's spell could hit me at any moment. My Jeep's tires made a lovely screeching noise as we pulled into the high-rise condo's parking garage, startling the attendant. Deval met us, which stopped said attendant from asking any questions as to why a turquoise Jeep, possibly now with now bald tires, had barreled into his domain.

I gave the irritated man an apologetic smile while Deval pulled his cousin from my passenger seat. Walking into the lobby, Vegard leaned heavily on Deval. The doorman's mouth thinned. *This is why you shouldn't live in a snooty building,* I thought, grateful that I could often avoid judgment while entering my home, unless of course the neighbors were out. I was a witch, after all.

Deval must have also seen the doorman's displeasure. "My cousin attended a bachelor party and forgot that his stamina isn't what he used to be," Deval offered as an explanation.

The doorman then directed his gaze at me. The leer in his eyes indicated that he thought I'd been the entertainment. He received a return glare from me. I almost zapped him before Deval spoke again.

"And this is a friend of the family, Ms. Darrow. She may be in and out this evening. I'm sure playing nursemaid to my cousin wasn't in her plans for the evening. Have a good evening, John."

"Very good, Mr. Rouge. Have a good evening." His previous sneer replaced by a cold facade.

I rolled my eyes and followed Deval to the elevator, the tension thick in the air while we waited. I needed to call Lola. I'd just left her in the chaos of fleeing. I didn't think that Michael would hurt her. He had an end game. I just didn't know what it was.

The elevator finally arrived, letting out a cheerful ping as its doors opened. An older, sophisticated-looking couple stepped out. Taking in Vegard's ashen appearance as he leaned heavily on Deval, the corners of their mouths pinched, but they moved quickly out of our way. Deval maneuvered his cousin in and with one hand fumbled around in his pocket before handing me a key card.

"Entering your building is like entering a judgmental gauntlet," I muttered taking the card.

Deval ignored my comment. "Hit the penthouse button and swipe the card."

It took a moment for me to register that, but I caught up quickly. "What, no retina scans? No blood test? Not even a ward? How disappointing," I needled Deval as I followed his instructions. Nervous sweat had started to bead my skin. I wasn't sure if it was because of Deval or because of the dirty magic that I could feel coursing under my skin. My stomach churned. No doubt Vegard felt that ten times worse.

"There is a healer here to help. I will ask that you keep her identity to yourself. She has in the past saved your own life, so I hope that you will respect that wish." Deval again completely ignored my attempt at humor. Spoilsport.

The doors opened into the condo before I could respond. Breathtaking nighttime views from the large banks of windows assaulted me, but they didn't keep my attention long. My magic, on alert, notified me of another witch in the room: the mystery healer.

A small pixie-like redhead appeared as I heard the elevator doors close behind me.

"Get him on the chaise," she ordered.

Deval deposited Vegard without any argument.

The redhead's turned to me. "There's some bad magic in you."

My gaze rested on her cool gray eyes. "It's not mine," I said. If she hadn't been a healer, I would have been affronted by her scanning me on that level without permission.

She gave me a brisk nod. "Are you able to remove it yourself?"

"Yes," I answered.

Another quick nod, and she turned her attention to Vegard.

My shields should have been up anyway, but I'd felt safe with Deval. Stupid, probably, but we had a history. He might drive me nuts, but he'd saved my life twice, and I didn't forget that. Of course, I'd found a thief for him and now worked for his mother, so the scales had started to even out.

A wave of nausea hit me. The adrenaline from fleeing the bar abandoned me, leaving only the sickly magic that crawled under my skin. I vaguely remembered a bathroom in the condo, and I fled in that direction.

"It's the second door on your right," Deval called from behind me.

I made it, barely. The porcelain was cool on my fore-arms as I retched into the toilet. A large hand began rubbing up and down my back in a soothing manner as my physical body tried to rid itself of the toxic spell. It wasn't until I had dry heaved for another five minutes that my body calmed.

I stood, flushing the toilet. The hand that had been the quiet calm in the ordeal removed itself. I staggered to the sink, turning on the faucet to rinse out my mouth and splash some cool water on my face. I began to shake, and I leaned forward relying on the granite countertop to support my weight. When I looked up, I met Deval's eyes in the mirror. Without a word, he picked me up and carried me out of the bathroom.

Normally, I'd have argued, but I needed to save my strength. Deval walked through the living area. Glancing up, I saw that the healer was pulling an angry purple of thread from Vegard's chest. *Something to look forward to.*

Deval took me into the room I'd stayed in when I'd been injured a couple of months earlier. A flip of the switch revealed the heavy furniture and cream sheets I remembered. Instead of taking me to the bed, he took me over to a large chaise longue in the corner of the room. He set me down, and my hands brushed against the dark-blue velvet that covered the piece in tufted intervals.

Apparently, this household used chaises longues for healing. Not that I was complaining. It was soft and gave me a perfect angle on my upper body to angle my head to look at my stomach and chest where I could feel the foreign spell sliding around under my skin.

"Do you need anything?" Deval asked.

"Just willpower."

He smiled down at me. "Since that's a synonym of stubbornness, I have no doubt you have plenty." He left my side then, but he didn't go far, just perched himself on the corner of the bed ready to watch the show.

I could wait for the healer in the other room to finish with Vegard, but he'd had a much larger hit than I had, so it would be a while. Also, I felt the spell growing inside of me. That could just be paranoia, but paranoia was a strong motivator, so I cleared my mind and reached for my magic.

The foreign spell tried to hide itself from me, but Deval was right, I was stubborn. I scanned my body, and sure enough, the spell sat in my chest like a tangled, spiky ball of yarn, ugly and invasive. Taking a deep breath, I studied it and found an end.

My magic fought to grip the end. Once it captured it, the puzzle began. I teased the knot from my body inch by agonizing inch. Sweat poured off me, my teeth clenched, and I felt a slight tremble in my body from the burning pain of pulling the dark matter from me. I tried to keep the tremble under control because every movement brought on the needles of pain.

Once I had a good amount of the spell wrapped around one hand like a spool of thread, Deval made a quiet exit, returning with a mason jar filled with salt. He opened the jar and set it on a small side table beside me. I hadn't thought about what I would do with the nasty stuff when I began, just eager to get it over with, but a salt cleanse would do nicely, and then an even better idea came to mind. I kept my plan to myself and returned my focus to the task at hand.

What could have been hours or minutes later, I did a final scan of myself, probing inside my own body and mind for any hint of something foreign remaining. Satisfied at finding nothing, I then sat up and grabbed the jar with my empty hand, taking the wound-up spell and pushing it into the jar, quickly closing the lid in case the spell had any sense of sentience and could realize the danger. Jar lid on as tight as I could twist it, I shook the jar, whispering a purifying incantation. The spell shuddered, turning a light pink except for a few purple flecks still floating around, so I continued to shake the jar, making sure the magic was properly cleansed.

"Is it done?" I jumped a little and nearly lost my grip on the jar. Deval had been so quiet the entire process I'd forgotten about him. He laughed quietly at me.

"You try pulling dark magic from your own body and then tell me you wouldn't spook at an unexpected noise," I said, scowling at him.

That earned me a radiant smile. "I have been the victim of many such things. I will not argue with you, but I will say I would hide my reaction better."

"Whatever," I muttered, holding the jar up to the sconce on the wall and examining it closely. I could not detect a single hint of the malevolent magic. Just to be safe, I recited the purification incantation one more time. Deval didn't say anything but watched me work my magic. The various magical species didn't often perform their magic in front of one another. I'd have had the same fascinated look on my face if Deval would ever be so kind as to allow me to watch him practice.

Quickly, I unscrewed the lid, reached out with my hand, took the cleansed magic, and pushed it inside my mouth, letting the now pure magic to reabsorb into my body. Hands were suddenly on my shoulders, shaking me, and I dropped the jar that now only contained salt onto the plush carpet. I looked up at Deval.

"I'm not vacuuming up the salt," I told him.

He stopped shaking me, but his fingers still dug into my shoulders. He stared down at me, eyes hard. "What has possessed you to take that foul magic back into your body after you spent so long removing it? Are you possessed?" His last question sounded hopeful. He wanted a supernatural reason to explain my behavior.

I rolled my eyes at him and reached up to break his grip from my shoulders. "No, dummy, it's like a vaccine."

"I have never heard of such a thing." He released my shoulders and folded his arms, not breaking eye contact.

"So, if you haven't heard of it, it's not possible?"

He sighed. "No, but I am much older than you, and I make it my business to know these things."

"Well, it's a relatively new practice. And it's not fool-proof. It won't make one completely immune to the caster's magic, but it does add a level of protection since an individual's own magic is often reluctant to attack itself. I cleansed it twice; it was totally safe."

"Would Pammy agree with that assessment?"

"Ehhh." I didn't know Pammy's stance on the cool new magic science.

"I knew it. It's not tested. Do you have a death wish?"

"You really need to stop asking me that." My jaw clenched, which made it difficult to get the sentence out. "Pammy lets her fortunes make their own decisions. I'm not the untrained novitiate you knew six weeks ago."

Now it was his turn to roll his eyes. "Oh, I am sorry that you went away to camp and came back thinking you're invincible. You should realize by now that is not the way the world works. I can't always save you."

Stepping in close, I pointed at him. "I went to 'camp,' as you so snidely called it, so you wouldn't have to save me, and the program that I attended does not deserve your scorn. Tonight I saved your cousin from a malicious attack, getting injured in the process, and I still got him out of the club and to a healer. All the while that foul magic grew inside of me, Deval. Do you think just any witch could pull a tangled malicious spell from her own body? Let me answer that for you, 'no'." The pointing had turned into me poking him to stress each word.

He grabbed my hand, but I twisted it free and turning marched to the door to go check on Vegard. Deval followed at my heels. I ignored him, not wanting to continue our conversation.

In the living room, Vegard remained prone on the chaise while the healer mimicked what I had just done to myself. I approached, and she looked up from her task.

"All taken care of?"

"Of course," I said, steel in my voice, tired of being underestimated. My shields were back up to full force, so I noticed when she didn't scan me to verify. Damn right, someone respected my mad skills. "Can I help you?"

She nodded, returning her gaze to her patient. "This is taking longer than I had hoped, and as I'm sure you know, it's not a painless process."

"Does he need to go under?" Deval inquired from behind me.

"No, it's not that severe."

I'd learned recently that goblins could assist in putting each other under if they were injured enough, but it was only in the severe cases. It shouldn't have been a surprise that their healer knew that, but I'd had to beg for every drop of goblin knowledge, and I was part goblin. I had a plane and everything. I huffed out an annoyed breath and went to the other side of the chaise.

My body felt shaky after my ordeal, but Vegard looked one hundred times worse. His skin had already become grayer at the bar and now had turned a deeper shade with a sickly green undertone. His dinner jacket from earlier had been removed, and the dress shirt he wore was soaked in sweat. His eyes were tightly shut as the other witch continued to pull the magic out of him.

I reached in with my own power, looking for another end. This time I found it in seconds.

"I see that you've used the new vaccine technique. Clever."

I shot Deval a triumphant look, and he answered with a scowl. "Yes, it seemed wise given the situation."

She nodded again, returning her concentration to her work, and I did the same. The tangled magic loosened itself easily this time around and allowed me to surpass quickly what the healer had been able to pull. All the while, Vegard remained silent with gritted teeth and closed eyes. The pain must have ramped up with me working on him as well, *but as they say, better out than in.*

We met in the middle, the thread of magic pulled tight between our two entry points. If I hadn't consumed the magic, we would have had to pull one of spools of magic back through, still faster than one person doing all the unraveling. With my new awareness of the magic. I reached out testing the fibers before I snapped it in two. Vegard's body jerked as we pulled our respective ends free.

Deval returned once more with a jar of salt. I pushed the sticky threads off my hand and into the jar. I snorted when Deval quickly confiscated the jar. The look on his face brought on an eye roll before I could stop myself, which he ignored and turned to the woman who deposited her own catch.

"Millicent, this is Peg," he introduced the woman whom I'd worked with, side-by-side.

"Nice to meet you," she grumbled before turning to

Deval, giving him a glare to rival his own. "Did you need to say my name?"

He shrugged while putting the lid on the jar. "Do you think Peg will tell Pammy who you are? The sheriff already knows and turns a blind eye."

"There's no way," Millicent spluttered before I interrupted.

"There is definitely a way. Pammy is well informed of everything that happens in her domain." That included the greater Phoenix area and to some extent the rest of the state. Out of sight out of mind helped the outlier cities but did not make them immune.

Crossing her arms, she turned her gaze on me. "Is that so?"

My hands flew up in innocence. "Hey, now, I didn't say I knew firsthand that she knew about you, just that the woman is known for her secrets. If your secrets don't hurt her or break any laws, do you really think she cares?"

She blew out an aggravated breath and turned back to Vegard, running a scan to make sure that we had gotten it all. Deval and I stood there, awkwardly waiting for her to finish. Just when I'd contemplated skulking out, she straightened.

"He'll be fine. He just needs rest," she said to Deval before pointing at me. "And you, just because she might know doesn't mean that you need to advertise it."

"Your secret's safe with me," I placated the delusional witch.

Deval handed Millicent the jar to dispose of, and she walked out of the room. To the bathroom, kitchen, secret sex dungeon, I didn't care because now that the crisis had passed, I needed to reach out to Lola.

Even though it was well after midnight by the time I'd extracted myself from Deval's home, I called Lola as soon as I sat in my Jeep. I needed to hear her voice, make sure she was okay.

Lola answered after several rings. "Gawds, Peg, why are you calling me so late? You ditched me!"

"Are you alone?"

"Of course, I am. I work tomorrow."

"Lola, I didn't ditch you. Vegard and I were attacked the minute you went to the bathroom."

There was a beat and then worry replaced the irritation in her voice. "Oh my god, Peg. I'm so sorry. Did the humans realize you were a witch?" Humans were known for their recreational witch bashing, so I could understand her jumping to that conclusion.

"No, Lo," I used her nickname to maybe soften the blow. "Michael threw a dirty spell at Vegard, and I caught some of the ricochet. We've been at Deval's getting healed."

The line had gone silent. Understandable, it was a lot to take in.

I let the silence drag for thirty seconds before tentatively asking, "Lo?"

"You're unbelievable. What has gotten into you? Accusing sweet Michael of such a horrible thing. He took care of me tonight when I cried about you leaving me to go have some tryst with another goblin."

I heard venom in her voice that had never been directed at me. My body tensed at the emotional onslaught. "I would never do that, Lola. You know that."

"After this stunt, I'm not really sure I'd know what you'd do at all, Peg." The line went dead.

6

In high school and college, I'd worked odd jobs with even odder schedules. After graduating, I figured I'd end up teaching, but since that hadn't fully come to pass, I'd never worked anything similar to the classic nine-to-five. Heretofore, I'd never understood all the animosity toward Monday, but now it was Monday, and Monday was the absolute worst. I finally had a case of the Mondays.

My foul mood had more to do with Lola's accusations than my waking up early, though that certainly didn't help. I made an entire pot of coffee, extra strong because it was too early for tequila, and I needed some liquid courage to back up the "give no fucks" attitude I'd awoken with.

At the kitchen table, motor oil in hand, I made the call. Not to Lola because frankly I didn't have time for an intervention. I would get to that later.

Deval answered on the second ring. "Peg." He managed to combine a statement and a question in my name.

"Yep, I need to come by your place."

"If you must, I'll tell the doorman to let you up."

"Uh, uh, I need to come to *your* place," I stressed the "your."

He paused for a moment. "That is more difficult."

"If your mama let me into her place, I don't see why you would have any objections. She hired me to find out how Grant stole George from right under your nose. You should have brought me over when that happened. I didn't push it because all the 'me goblin, you witch,' bullshit, but apparently I'm a witchlin, so this is getting ridiculous."

"Witchlin?"

"Combination of witch and goblin."

"No, I understood that part; I just don't know why you'd ever deliberately christen yourself as one."

I took another gulp of coffee before responding. "I've been called worse. Now who's picking me up, and should I bring my own hood?"

"Hood?"

"Don't play dumb. We both know you're going to blindfold me." I didn't have the patience for this garbage today.

"True, I just did not think you to be the type to own a hood," he replied, deadpan.

"I don't, but I have a sleeping mask that should suffice."

"Then why did you offer?" He sounded genuinely curious.

I slammed my coffee mug down, causing the hot liquid to slosh over my hand. I bit the inside of my cheek to stop from cursing.

"Are you breaking things, Peg?"

"Nope, that was Cheddar," I lied glibly.

"Uh huh."

Okay, apparently not as glib as I had thought. "I offered to bring my own hood as a way to expedite this process. We both know what it will take to get this trail ride trotting, and I, believe it or not, have several things on my plate. Who is picking me up and when?"

"Fine, I will collect you within the hour. You are in a foul mood today, Peg."

"It's Monday," I growled into the phone before ending the call.

A few days ago, I'd have put more effort into my appearance at the prospect of seeing Deval. At this point, I'd come to the conclusion that romantic interests were stupid and dangerous. Case in point, Lola's obsession with Michael and Fane's obsession with me. Dangerous. Ratty jeans, a V-neck, and flip-flops were good enough for my day-to-day, and they were good enough for Deval. Being able to wear flip-flops in December was a winter privilege I had earned by driving my car wearing oven mitts in the Arizona summer.

A knock on my front door came thirty minutes later. Good thing, too. I'd been considering adding some Grand Marnier to my coffee. Not my most professional idea. I opened the door without checking the peephole or my wards. My mood that would not let up practically dared anyone to try to mess with me.

Deval stood on my front porch. Hair pulled back, gray T-shirt, jeans, and boots. "Ready to go?"

"Yep, I see that you got the memo about casual day."

His gaze moved over me taking in my messy ponytail, well-worn outfit, and finally stopped at my footwear.

"What?"

"I went casual. You went one step above hobo."

I rolled my eyes. "You just can't handle the flop." Where had that come from?

"Oh, I can handle the flop. I never said you weren't an attractive hobo."

My stomach did a little flip. "Uh huh, you're just being nice because my bad mood is frightening you."

He scoffed. "I am not frightened by you."

"Well, maybe you should be." I crowded him out of my doorway, closing the front door and locking it with my back to him. He only gave me enough room to complete my task, allowing no extra space. Apparently, he needed to prove that he indeed lacked any fear in association with me. If I rolled my eyes anymore, I suspected that my face might get stuck that way.

"Can we go through a Dutch Bros drive through?" I asked when we were seated in his car, a sedan that was large, comfy, and luxury.

He looked over, scowling. "Is this a field trip for you?"

"Of course not," I snapped. "I take this very seriously, which is why I need something that has sugar and coffee. It will make me alert, and for your benefit, I guarantee that I'll be nicer having consumed it."

"I don't mind your mood."

I looked over at him frowning. He liked me when I was this salty? I shook my head, nope, not even thinking about it. "I mind my mood; it takes a lot of energy to be this snarky. Please." I grated.

He sighed. "Direct me to this Dutch Bros."

I grinned like a loon at him and gave him instructions.

The hood didn't make an appearance until after we'd gone through the drive-through. This time around, I didn't fall asleep on the journey. Instead I sipped happily on thirty ounces of heaven through a straw. I made a mental note to require a large beverage with an equally large straw any time I was whisked away to super-secret goblin land.

Happily caffeinated, I noted that we spent the majority of our journey on the highway before eventually hitting a dirt road. This part I remembered. The only things I heard were the classical music, something Eastern European and robust, and the ping-ping of gravel crunching under the tires and shooting up into the undercarriage. Deval stayed decidedly mum throughout the trip. Fine by me. I didn't feel particularly chatty.

The car finally came to a stop, and I waited until Deval came around. I knew the drill from the last time. My door opened, and the crisp December air startled me a little. I guessed that we were at one of the mountain ranges that surrounded Phoenix, and the air was cooler up here. Sharp pebbles dug into the foam of my sandals. Yep, that little rebellion had been a stupid choice. I held out my hand and quickly felt Deval's cool grasp encompassing it.

"What do you want me to do with this?" I held out the empty cup wiggling it in what I hoped was his face to show it empty. He'd probably figured that out when I'd made a few unladylike slurps at the end of the liquid heaven.

"Put it in a trash can."

Cup still in hand I motioned to my currently covered face. "If I can't see a trash can, I can't use it, can I? Say that five times fast."

He ignored my tongue twister challenge. "Can't you scan for one?"

"Seriously, Deval? Do you really think trash cans have magical auras?"

He grumbled something but took the empty cup. I felt ridiculously pleased at the exchange, since I'd come out ahead. Sugar and caffeine had a way of making small victories feel more epic than they actually were.

We did the "lead me through the rocks and gravel stumble dance" that Griselda introduced me to last time, and, well, I stumbled. Just like at his mother's, Deval eventually stopped me and began a chant. The magic rose quickly, and this time it reached out to me to whisper in my ear. I didn't speak goblin, so I didn't know what it said, but it felt welcoming like wading into a warm lake. Gravel paths once again turned to smooth stone, and the headgear was removed.

This cavern was smaller than his mother's, but it still displayed the high ceilings studded with dramatic stalactites. Among them hung an ornate copper chandelier with ever-burning candles, casting light to bring out the different patterns in the stone that surrounded us. Carpets and sofas in designs interspersed with cobalt blue and deep brown made the room feel luxurious and cozy at the same time; all of the furniture was in pristine condition. That was odd because the room held the slight damp and metallic taste that were characteristic of caves and mines. Magic was at work for sure.

"How do you like it?" he asked.

I looked up at him, surprised that he cared what I thought. "I suppose it's kinda nice."

"Kinda nice?"

"I mean my jeans would mold as soon as I got them out of the dryer. Is there even a laundry room?" I looked around, noting two hallways oddly arranged in the corners farthest from me.

"Of course there's a laundry room, and nothing molds in here...you're joking." He finally noticed my grin.

"As if you didn't know that your home was stunning.

You don't need your ego to get any larger. So where was George?"

"My mother told me you named it that," he said softly.

"And here I thought Delmy and I shared a secret."

"You've mentioned George twice now. Why would you if you considered it a secret?"

Good question. Delmy had after all told me to keep my goblin plane's name to myself. "Well, since you bought him, I thought you'd want to know his name even if he likes me better than you."

"He does; gods know why." He shook his head.

"You liked me well enough at one point."

His eyebrows pinched as he looked at me quizzically. "Are we having this discussion?"

I shook my head no. "Nope, there is work to be done." I broke eye contact, looking around the room.

"And you don't want to deal with it." His fingers touched my chin to bring my gaze back to his, but it was a statement and not a question. He searched my face briefly and then released me.

I held back the shivers until he looked away and let one tremor shake my body. Maybe I did want to deal with it, but not today.

"George was placed right here." Deval went and stood between two massive dark wood shelves.

My gaze drifted briefly over eclectic collection of titles before turning to the place of honor neatly made between them. "You planning on commissioning another one?" I asked, curious.

"No."

"Why not?" I had probably hit on some sort of goblin faux pas. Was asking about the number of planes one owned the goblin equivalent of asking how much money they made?

Deval folded his arms. "This is not something we talk about lightly."

Nailed it in one.

"But since you are new to our culture, I will humor you."

"Please do." I inclined my head.

"Our realms or planes are sentient, which you must know because you have given yours a name. Mine, too, has a name, and realms can be finicky about having another in their domain."

"Interesting. I thought that more realms equaled more power. I assumed that powerful goblins held more than one."

"Some do, but some, like mine, may force another out and expand to accommodate their owner's wishes."

"Do you actually own them then, or could they turn on you?"

"Like George left me for you?"

"Well, I didn't want to mention it, but let's be honest, I have a sunnier disposition."

He chuckled. "No doubt, but it is a symbiotic relationship. Our presence breathes life into our realms, and they return it. 'Own' is simply a convenient word. In truth it is more of a marriage of magic."

"My mother will be so thrilled."

"Why?"

"She always wanted me to get married." I couldn't keep the grin off my face at my own stupid joke.

Deval groaned. "That is akin to saying that you love Cheddar, so why don't you marry him."

"What can I say? I'm unusually giddy and feeling silly after all that coffee."

"If I didn't know better, I'd think Dutch Bros put something in your drink."

I folded my arms and looked at Deval. "You preferred the angry version?"

"I told you, Peg, I like all versions of you, oddly enough. No one is more surprised by this development than I."

I locked eyes with him. "Liking you is also disconcerting."

He took a step closer. "You admit to liking me?" I turned, giving him my back and began to study the walls surrounding the area the theft had taken place. Deval didn't take the hint and stepped right behind me, his breath tickling my ear. "I'll take that as a 'yes' then."

Shrugging dismissively wasn't as effective when said shoulders ran into a hard chest. A shiver went through me, but before he could call me on it, I turned, shooing at him with my hands. "Back up, buddy, I have magic to do."

Deval backed away from me, sighing.

"Do you want to leave the room while I search?"

"I would not leave you unattended." He took a seat in a chair positioned in the corner of the room, leaned back, and folded his arms and crossed his ankles, watching me."

Talk about killing the mood. "Where's the trust?"

"Not here yet."

I managed to keep from wincing, but that stung a little. After all, I'd let him into my plane. Technically it had been his but still according to all knowledgeable sources that was a rather intimate thing to do, and he wasn't even willing to leave me alone in his living room for thirty minutes. I shook my head to dislodge the angry feelings that were beginning to surface. Once I had centered myself, I reached out with my magic.

I started at the corner near the entrance. My magic reached out in tendrils to slowly touch every wall, knick-knack, tchotchke, rug, book, speck of dust, anything else physically in the room. Slowly and steadily, I searched for that reactive spark of magic greeting magic. I'd been prepared to go over the room with a fine-toothed comb, so to speak, so feeling that zing five minutes later came as a surprise.

"There." I pointed up to a tapestry that hung from one of the walls. It appeared to be from the Middle Ages and likely was. The colorful cloth showed a king looking over his feast. The magic emanated from the figure's crown. If the person that placed the magic was trying to send a message, they were anything but subtle.

Deval rose and walked toward the tapestry. "What am I looking for, exactly?"

"The crown." I walked forward to stand by him. "Is there anything different at all? A speck of dust, a drop of blood, anything?"

"Well, there's a small gold bead attached. Considering that this is not a beaded rug, I'd say that's different." His voice was dry, betraying no emotions.

Yeah, having your home invaded sucked. I stepped forward to take a closer look. The bead was tiny and blended in well with the gold of the fabric. I turned to look at Deval. "Is the bead real gold?"

"You should be able to tell that," he referenced my new and exciting goblin heritage.

"Not so much. My only goblin skill seems to be that I can walk into George." Well, and be healed by George and given a super boost of energy, but Deval didn't need to know everything. Man wouldn't even leave me alone in his damn living room.

His look suggested that he wasn't buying my lack of powers line, but he continued. "It is. I'm surprised they would use gold for their spell. Since I can detect it much as a shark can detect blood."

I pointed at his watch; it was heavy, gold, and some expensive brand that was so exclusive that I had no idea what it was. "Can being in the presence of other gold dull that sense?"

"Of course."

"Why would you think twice about a speck of gold in your room?"

His jaw clenched while he thought this over. After a minute of waiting for him to speak, I turned back to the crown and let a tiny tendril of magic sweep over the bead. It wasn't active, but it wasn't dormant either. I probed a little deeper. Ah, a scrying focus. It would make Deval's home easy to monitor when needed, but as it was only a focus; it didn't need to be fully powered, which meant it could avoid detection for long periods of time.

"You're right. I never would have noticed it."

Caught up in analyzing the scrying focus, I jumped when Deval spoke.

"I should keep better track of every speck of gold I own, and where it resides. I blame old age and complacency. I never would have noticed this thing if you hadn't scanned and found it."

I didn't comment because aging was a touchy subject. I considered telling him that I'd had to use Urban Dictionary to look up "ratchet" a few years ago, so I knew his pain. I doubted, however, that he would get the reference, so I kept it to myself. "Do you perform any regular security checks in here?"

"Annually."

"Same time every year?" I prodded.

"Yes." He gritted his teeth.

"When last year?"

"January."

Great, someone could have been spying on Deval for

an entire year. Longer, if whoever did Deval's check was incompetent.

"What is it exactly that this bead would do? It's not as though it's a hidden camera, and it is too small to hold much magic."

I nodded. "It's a focus for a scrying spell."

"How can you tell?"

"I just can." I shrugged. "Different magics have different tones. I worked quite a bit on scrying spells at the boot camp. They're a really great surveillance system. Someone drops a little something intoned with magic, and then someone can check in periodically. The good news for you is that the spell doesn't work for sound, only visuals."

A vein I never noticed before started to throb against his temple. "Visuals could be enough."

I looked more closely at the bead, which was actually more of a flake. Had they Superglued it on? That would just be the cherry on this invasion of privacy sundae. Don't just spy on a man in his super-secret lair, also defile his fancy antique wall hanging. I decided not to debate the different methods that might have been used to set this anchor.

"Do you mind if I do another sweep?" Better to be thorough.

"If you must." Deval walked purposefully to one of his chairs and sat, hands gripping the armrests. Anger rolled off him although he kept his face passive. *Yep, really pissed.*

Subtly, this time around felt unnecessary, and I let my magic pour forth, coating the space, but doing my best to contain it to this room. The gate to his plane was in here, so there was no need to be nosy even if curiosity gnawed at me. Taking a deep breath, I cleared my mind and removed my focus from the watchful man. I searched the room once more. Magic lived in the room, but Deval had a particular signature, and after a few minutes, I could say that there were only two other signatures in the room. One belonged to the scrying focus and the other belonged to the plane.

About to pull the magic back to me, it suddenly had a will of its own, surging forward to the chest that served as the gate to Deval's plane.

"Whoa, whoa, whoa," I mumbled as Deval surged to his feet. I yanked on my magic, bringing it back to myself, but it brought along a friend. Goblin magic surrounded me, singing the same siren song that George had used to coax me into visiting him. That last time, I'd been unable to stop myself from accepting that invitation and had nearly frozen to death, being unused to the conditions of goblin planes. This time around, I didn't want to travel into another magical dimension. I wanted Deval, now.

The euphoria and desire that suddenly pulsed through me had me turning, about to pounce on the object of my desire. Before I'd taken a single step, Deval lifted me and shoved me against a wall. My mind briefly wondered how he'd gotten over to me so quickly but halted completely when he nuzzled my neck, stubble scratching at my skin. He moved his mouth higher and bit my ear.

I threw my arms around his neck and wrapped my legs around his waist. I couldn't get close enough, and the friction was *so good*. His mouth abandoned my ear, and his eyes met mine as he leaned in and bit my lower lip. I sucked in a quick breath before his mouth covered mine. Before I'd been a little too shocked, overcome with magic, to be an active participant, but his tongue slid against my lips, and my desire finally caught up with his.

His hands gripped my ass, and I managed to pull him even closer as he rocked his body against mine. I began to wonder if I'd ever breathe again and decided that it didn't matter when Deval suddenly pulled away from me. I nearly fell but managed to brace myself against the wall. The magic that had flooded the room thick and hazy shot back into its respective owners. My magic hit me hard, and my knees buckled a little.

The desire remained, but it had dampened to manageable levels. I didn't want to look at Deval, so I bent over, hands on my knees and took a few deep breaths. A few moments later, when I found the courage to look Deval in the eyes, I wasn't prepared for the equal parts fear and awe I saw there. Why would he fear me?

"Well, uh, that isn't part of my usual security check, so please don't tell your mom."

His brows drew together. "I don't share intimate details of my life with my mother."

"Me, neither," I lied. "Uh, so that was odd. Is your plane also your wingman? I'll have to tell George he's been slacking."

Deval just stared at me. "I think it's best if I return you to your home."

Guess my attempt at humor to alleviate the tension had failed. We stood awkwardly for a few moments. "Okay, I really do need to come back though. With preparation, I may be able to reverse the scry."

"We will make those arrangements. Please gather your things."

Deval turned formal when he wanted to avoid something. I debated asking him what the hell all that had been, but frankly, I felt drained: magically, emotionally, physically, but not so much sexually, and that was a bother.

7

Being left in front of my house, hot and bothered, after a very silent drive home with quite possibly the sexiest man I had known while blindfolded, really made me wonder about my life choices. Especially when he peeled away from my curb like a bat out of hell.

I stared at the black sedan until it turned off my road and shook my head. I noticed a neighbor had come outside to glare at me from her front porch. A little wave from me had her turning to march back inside. I didn't advertise myself as a witch for the most part, but I wasn't closeted, and some people thought I'd brought down the property values even though my aunt, another witch, had owned this house for a decade before me.

Nothing like a micro-aggression to kill the mood; oh wait, it was probably being rejected faster than a counter-feit bill at a bank that had done that. Two things would make it better: coffee and George. My new pick-me-up usually worked even better than me trying to cuddle Cheddar into submission only to end up slightly bloody for all of my trouble. Cheddar was a simple cat. Snuggles were rare and on his schedule.

An hour later, and I had reached peak magic and caffeine levels thanks to my new ritual, but it didn't take the edge off the turmoil churning in my gut. I wanted to gab with Lola, but when I called, she sent me directly to voicemail. Anger and worry did not make a good combination. When on the outs with one friend, it helped to have a backup. Bruce, a bear shifter of Pima or Akimel O'odham origin, picked up on the second ring.

"Good looking, I thought you'd forgotten about me," he answered a mournful tone in his voice.

"I've only been home a few days."

"After being gone six weeks, I'd expect a call within forty-eight hours."

"Sorry, things have gone haywire, and you got bumped to the seventy-two-hour group," I teased.

"Ouch, I'd be hurt, but if you say things have gone haywire since picking up the fortune gig, I tend to assume you're fighting off vampires, reversing treacherous curses, and trying to knit your cat a sweater, all in the same weekend."

"I tried to knit a cowl one time, and it wasn't for Cheddar." I thought back to the beautiful skein of yarn I'd purchased along with the needles. After watching a few tutorials, I'd dived into what turned out to be a bundle of tangles, knots, and missed stitches that ended up in a forgotten drawer where crafts went to die.

One day, Bruce had been over for dinner, and Cheddar somehow managed to open said drawer using his kitty genius and had run through the living room in full Halloween cat mode, tangled in the burnt-orange yarn, needles trailing behind him. Bruce still insisted I'd been attempting to knit a sweater onto a live feline. And, I might be willing to visit the occasional vampire if work called for it, but I wasn't suicidal.

"Uh huh." He dropped it, though I could hear the chuckle he wanted to let loose in his voice. "You inviting me to lunch?"

"I'm that easy to read?" I asked.

"Nope, I'm just hungry and decided to use reverse psychology on you."

"Well, it worked, Rosa's?"

"Thirty minutes?"

"Deal."

The strip mall Mexican restaurant was decked out in the traditional decor of bright colors, heavy wooden furniture, and Saltillo tile, and smelled like heaven. I'd beaten Bruce there because, despite my senior citizen preference for driving styles, I lived much closer. Seated at a booth in a corner, I gorged on chips and salsa while I waited. The waiter graciously provided a second basket of chips and a new container of salsa to hide my crime, just before Bruce strolled in.

He came to my booth, his shockingly white smile gorgeous against his copper skin. His dark hair, about an inch long, stood out at random intervals, unsurprising given his penchant to shave his head when he got sick of dealing with his hair, letting it grow out to an unruly length and then starting the process all over again.

He stopped next to the bench I sat on. "Well, get up and give me a real greeting, and I'll forget that you waited three days to call me."

I stood, and he enveloped me in a hug before lifting me and twirling me twice for good measure to the amusement of the patrons seated at the handful of tables, who had come in for a late lunch. After he set me down, we settled in the booth across from each other.

"Joke's on you, buster. You could sell those hugs as instant therapy, and I got one for free." I winked at him.

His smile grew impossibly brighter. "How much do you think I could sell them for?"

"Easily five bucks each. You work an eight hour shift, you'll be rolling in it, and you can take me to the Bahamas, or better yet, someplace cooler when it hits one-twenty."

"I'll take you and Lola wherever you ladies wanna go. I'll look like a real ladies' man."

The mention of Lola sucked the cheer right out of me, and I focused on the fresh basket of chips.

"What's going on?" he prodded.

I swallowed. "Things are a little rocky with me and Lola right now. She's gotten caught up with some bad people and won't listen to sense."

Our waiter appeared, and we ordered: shrimp tacos topped with pineapple salsa for me and tamales smothered in green chile salsa for him. After the waiter left, I unloaded the whole story about Michael, what his family did, Lola's tentative childhood tie, and I finished it off with a rant about my encounter with Deval earlier that morning. When I finally came up for air and shoved yet another tortilla chip in my mouth, Bruce let out a long whistle.

"Damn girl. This isn't the first basket of chips that came to this table is it?"

I flushed a little at my penchant for stress eating and grabbed another chip. Mouth full, I responded, "Nope, and it's not likely to be the last one, either."

He nodded. "We'll get you some fried ice cream, too, if you promise you'll be capable of getting some work done afterwards because, girl, you've got a pile of shit and a shovel, and you know what you need to do."

"Do I though?"

"Don't be an idiot. Priority numero uno: get some dirt on that family. Lola's not safe but you'll keep a look out for her. Then you gotta do your job. Money may not be the answer to everything, but it sure is nice to be able to eat. Finally, don't you worry about Deval; that will work itself out. He's just scared cuz he's found his queen."

I choked on a chip and had a coughing fit as the jagged little piece tried to invade my airway.

"What? You gonna act like there ain't chemistry?"

I grabbed my water and gulped it down when I could breathe again, and then I set the glass on the table with a thud. "Of course there is. I don't make out with just anyone, but a strong sexual chemistry does not lend itself to queen status."

"No, but his safe calling to you would."

"How do you know it was the safe?"

He gave me the ol' "do I look stupid to you" look. "They act like it's a big secret but any supernatural who's over fifty knows about it."

"Lola acted like it was a state secret." My mouth pinched in annoyance.

"Well, she's under fifty, and like I said, goblins try to keep it a secret, but it's like my uncle Lester. He's older than shit, so given society, we knew why he didn't come out, but he walked around hitting on any woman in sight as if we didn't all know his 'friend' Clarence wasn his partner, and frankly we didn't give a shit. Clarence is a great guy and a plumber. Do you know how convenient it is to have plumber in the family?"

"I think you may have gotten a little off topic here."

"Maybe, but it's a good analogy. Everybody knows that

Lester is gay, and everyone knows that the safes exist, and what they do. Doesn't mean that knowledge couldn't be dangerous for the people involved. Even though you and I don't care, there's always gonna be some asshole out there who's gonna gay bash or try to steal the source of a person's power."

Not a direct analogy but close enough that I didn't argue. Our food arrived, and we ate with purpose and in silence. Not speaking again until our plates were clean and the fried ice cream had been ordered.

Biting the bullet, I asked the question gnawing at my brain. "What do you mean his plane calling to me indicates that I'm his queen?"

"Well, if he weren't prince, the queen business would mean nothing. It's not the end all be all kismet that you two are meant to be together, but it does mean that your magic is compatible."

"Great, we'll get together and have a spell circle." Snark coated my voice.

"Don't go getting saucy with me, miss. Magic lives in your soul and is therefore influenced by it, be that good or bad. If you two have good juju, that should be something to celebrate."

I slumped in my seat. "That sounds wonderful until you remember the part where he couldn't get away from me fast enough. You should have seen how fast he pulled away from my house. There are skid marks to prove it." My voice had gotten shrill at the stark reminder of the callous rejection. "Besides, until you told me what it all meant, I just thought it was another playboy being an asshole. Now I'm being rejected by my magical soul mate." My eyes stung a little, but I tipped my head back and held off the unwanted tears.

Bruce reached across the table, and I rested my hand in

his warm strong grip. "Sweetheart, men as old as Deval get a little scared of the real deal. Give him time. But while you give him that time, you go and live your life. There are millions of souls, and just because one would be a good fit doesn't mean the timing or circumstance is right."

I managed a small smile to show Bruce that his words helped. The raw devastation that had hit me had a lot to do with all of the chaos that currently circled me, not just Deval. "I just wish I could talk to Lola about this."

"What am I? Chopped Liver?" It was hard to look affronted when a smile pulled at your lips, but Bruce did the best he could.

I gave his hand another squeeze before releasing it. "Nope, you sir, are the finest of meats. I'll get you a T-shirt that says so."

"I'd rather you didn't," he grimaced.

"But it could be your Christmas present," I protested.

"Tell you what, why don't you just give me a quick kiss under the mistletoe one of these nights instead."

"Deal." Ours was a platonic friendship, but a little flirt with an attractive man never hurt anyone, and I'd just saved myself twenty bucks on screen-printing.

"Now, I've been sitting here and thinking about what you told me about Lola, and I can't help but have a vague recollection of a nasty witch family bringing some trouble maybe twenty years ago."

I perked up, knowing the timing to be just right. Lola's parents had died when she was five, and she currently hit the quarter of a century mark.

"What can you remember about these people?"

"Not much and mostly rumors. I was in the rodeo circuit back then. Didn't have a lot of time to socialize outside those guys, but I do remember going home at one point and my mom saying there was some bad stuff brewing for the witches. New family in town causing trouble. Best I can remember, they ran before they could do much harm."

"Do you remember if your mom said why they ran?"

"About that time there was the power shift of Pammy taking over Arizona. Ambitious is an understatement, and whereas there may have been some missed items in the general turnover, you better believe that Pammy wouldn't have left any bad news witches to their own devices. She had a rep to make."

"Well, her rep has been made tenfold, so why would they risk coming back?"

"Did they try to hide their arrival?"

"No."

"Then they hedged the bet, thinking Pammy wouldn't connect the dots. She has, but they're still here. My guess is they left something behind, something worth the risk, or they're idiots who underestimate Pammy."

"My guess is both."

Our fried ice cream arrived, and while the combination of ice cream, cinnamon, and corn flakes topped with whipped cream and honey hit my tongue in what should have been a combination of ecstasy, I couldn't really enjoy it. I didn't know the reason, but the McAllisters had only pursued one connection since their arrival to my knowledge: Lola.

8

My Jeep was not the best vehicle for surveillance. Its bright color did not scream unremarkable. I'd inherited it from my dad and at the price of free. I couldn't complain, but in the hopefully near future, I'd need to purchase an old compact that wouldn't be so obvious on a stakeout.

After leaving Bruce behind, I'd called Pammy. Good news was she knew where the McAllisters were staying. Bad news was that they knew what she drove, since she'd had a very tense visit with the matriarch of the family. Which meant that when she asked me if I was in the mood for a stakeout, I couldn't ask to borrow her old Crown Victoria. Well, I could, but it felt counterproductive.

The street the McAllisters stayed on in East Mesa had a lot of traffic and a number of cars lined the street. I wedged my own between a F-250 and a Corolla, hoping to be overlooked in between the two unremarkable models. Stakeouts weren't fun, but they were a necessary evil of the job. I had foregone my usual evening Diet Pepsi, knowing that copious amounts of liquids did not equal a successful spy session with no restroom available. Not that there had been much to observe.

The two-story house lay in a development built in the nineties. The tan stucco house looked like all of the other tan stucco houses with the desert landscaping that consisted of rocks and a few spiny mesquite trees. The lights were turned on in the windows both upstairs and down. The family apparently hadn't heard of energy conservation. No one walked by the windows, and no lights flickered to indicate a television playing.

After two hours, it went from dusk to full twilight, and my eyes began to cross. It was like sitting in an art museum for hours, staring at the most tedious landscape. The only things that interrupted my adventure were slouching when a pedestrian walked by and shifting occasionally to wake an ass cheek that had fallen asleep only to have to shift a while later when the other had followed suit. To my shame, my eyes became harder and harder to keep open, which caused me to jump and let out a startled shriek when my passenger door suddenly opened. My magic pushed up so quickly I felt like I'd touched one of those toy buzzers kids hid in their hands.

"It's just me." Deval's cousin Vegard slid into my passenger seat and closed the door with the thud that accompanied older vehicles.

"Just me? Are you following me?" I wanted to sound like a cool and collected detective. Shrill fishwife would be a more accurate description.

"Obviously."

I swallowed and let my power brush out the tips of my fingers. Locked and loaded. "Whatever you have planned, I don't think you're ready to take me on."

"Take you on?" He looked down at my hands, which emitted a soft glow. "Whoa, I said I was following you, not that I planned on murdering you and feeding you to the pigs."

"Pigs?" My face scrunched up.

"Haven't you ever seen *Snatch*?"

I suddenly recalled the scene in the movie. "Yes, but still that's a bit morbid. What exactly can I do for you since you claim to have no interest in feeding me to the pigs?"

"I'm here to help you."

"Help me what?"

"With your inquiry into my family."

I just stared at him for a moment. "And you've been just sitting in this neighborhood watching me for hours to help?" *Because that wasn't creepy.*

"Okay, so when you parked here I didn't realize how long you'd be here, so I decided to bite the bullet and just approach you. I love my father and brother, but their ideas have become somewhat off lately. I want there to be a peaceful resolution before they go too far."

"Like stealing from the heir to the goblin throne?"

Vegard winced.

"So, they did do it?"

"I have no proof, but I would bet money on it." He sighed.

"You have no proof, but you're here to help?"

He suddenly grabbed my hand. I dampened my magic, not wanting to hurt the guy. *Dear gods, please don't let me become pig feed.*

"I can help. I've distanced myself over the years because, frankly, they're not stable. I wonder now if that's been a mistake. If I'd maintained a closer relationship, would they have taken it this far?"

I looked into his eyes, and while they looked earnest, I hesitated.

"Look, I'm going to go and try to rebuild my relationship with my family. I want this to end peacefully. I doubt they can get away with what they've done, what they're no doubt planning to do next, but I'm hoping to lighten the blow. Make them see reason. If they can just apologize to Aunt Delmy, I have no doubt that she'll forgive them in century or two. We can wait, but not if they're dead or in some hole of a plane left without any gold to rot away the rest of their lives."

"So, that's what's wrong with the American prison system, there's no gold." Snark only mildly coated my voice. "So, tell me, what would you do differently this time that you haven't in the past? If you're that far out, will they even let you into the fold? Why risk yourself now?"

"They've gone too far this time. It's borderline treason, and I love my entire family. That includes Delmy and Deval. They've always been good to me. I don't know what I can do differently, but I have to try."

"I get that, but what can I possibly do to help you? I'm looking to prove they're guilty. Not stage a family intervention."

He nodded and pulled his hand away from mine. "I know that, but I figured if I came to you and offered my help that you might ask for leniency on their behalf. I will as well, of course, but your opinion would help tremendously."

"Oh, sweetheart, you are in for a rude awakening if you think I hold any type of sway over the goblin monarchy."

"That's untrue. You are at the very least a novelty, a treasured child who has sprung from the stone in a time of darkness. Our people miss the relationships the supernatural communities once nurtured before those trials and all the destruction they brought. At best, however, you are of interest to Deval, and given what he has been prone to in the past, I have no doubt that Delmy is rubbing her hands together at the prospect that Deval is bringing home a warrior rather than a woman whose current life focus is who she can get to spring for the latest trendy bag."

"Novelty maybe, but warrior definitely not. Last fight I was in left me bleeding out until Deval came to the rescue." I rolled my eyes.

"Did you manage to stave off two powerful beings?"

"Eh, really, I just managed not to die."

"Well, that's more than most can do, and you're young. It's already rumored that you're Pammy's ingénue, and that she is grooming you."

I reached over and covered Vegard's mouth with my hand. "Gods almighty, don't you say things like that. One, she'll hear about it and assume I'm looking to take her out and murder me herself, or two, even scarier, you're right. I'd be a terrible sheriff." I removed my hand and leaned back against the driver's door, trying to distance myself from the very idea of that much power and responsibility. More like that much headache and an early grave to show for it.

"Hence, why I said the 'grooming.' The old witch has some good years left in her, but there's nothing wrong with a retirement plan."

"I'm not even Catholic," I said as I crossed myself. "If you stop telling me that I'm the heir apparent to the Arizona witches, I'll promise to recommend leniency, should it turn out that your father or brother had anything to do with the theft of the safe."

"They did. I just have no proof." The weight of the sadness in his words hit me. He really just wanted to try to lighten the punishment that no doubt hung over his family's heads. Not a burden I wanted to bear.

"Get proof. You're always in a better position to

bargain if you have something to offer. I'm sure Delmy would be willing to listen to you. You're family after all."

"What is the modern term?" he asked his face lightening with a small smile, "You're just blowing smoke up my ass."

I cocked my head. "Damn right, I'm just blowing smoke up your ass. Dude, if you think I hold any sway, you're highly mistaken, but if possible, coming to the market with wares to sell is better than coming with a cup to beg. Of course, sometimes you need to beg. I'd be prepared for that if I were you."

He quieted, looking contemplative.

I turned my body to face the house and give him a moment with his thoughts. Shocking, nothing had changed. Lights on but no movement. I sighed.

"My brother and father are not in that house." Vegard turned in his seat as well to look out the windshield.

"How would you know?"

"I would feel them. I've been sitting out here as long as you have been."

I shrugged. "They're not who I'm looking for tonight."

"Who are you looking for?"

"The witch who threw the dirty magic at us."

He folded his arms and settled further in his seat. "Tonight just got more interesting."

I glanced at him before returning my eyes to the house. Lord knew what I might have missed while we had our tête-à-tête. "Believe me when I say that tonight just got the opposite of interesting."

"Not a fan of the stakeout?"

"Not a fan of fluid restriction and my ass falling asleep."

He nodded. "Those are the bad parts. As you get older it becomes somewhat meditative, relaxing even."

I stifled a yawn behind my hand. "Oh, old one, tell me about my wasted youthful ways."

He chuckled and faced forward. He probably would have gone into a meditative state, too, if Lola hadn't marched out of the house, looking madder than a cat in a bathtub, well, except for that one freak of nature kitten on the Internet.

I ducked down and then realized how ridiculous that appeared, considering my Jeep and the fact that she beelined straight for us, so instead I gave little wave. Her fists were clenched at her sides, and she somehow marched harder, a West Point level of aggressiveness to her marching.

"You were spying on Lola?" Vegard asked under his breath.

"Nope, just the bad apple family she's been associating with."

"I've heard of over-protective parents, but this is a whole new level for a friend."

"Rumor has it that they're drainers."

He hissed in a breath. "I'll hold her; you bind her. We'll stash her away until Pammy gets the family to move on, preferably to the other side."

I looked at him. "Don't tempt me."

"Why not?"

I thought about it. Lola was still about fifty feet from the car. "She'd never forgive me, and I believe, no, hope that she's going to see reason. Plus, I think Pammy is using her as bait, and as much as that gives me hives, I do believe that Pammy knows what she's doing."

"She'll choose the health of the coven over the health of a single witch."

My gut churned. I knew that, but I also knew that I'd look out for Lola. Proof being that I stayed in my seat while my best friend approached, looking angrier than I'd ever seen her, instead of peeling away from the curb and fleeing like a yahoo.

Swallowing, I rolled down my window with the mechanical crank. "Oh, hey, Lola, I didn't expect to see you tonight."

"What in god's name are you doing? Are you spying on Michael? This is so low, Peg, even for you."

My brain froze as I tried to come up with an excuse.

"She's meeting me. I had a few things to discuss with her. You know, goblin business." *Smooth, Vegard, smooth.*

Lightning flashed in Lola's eyes, like literal lightning; she was so angry her powers were creeping up. "Goblin business, my ass. I'm a bloody goblin for all intents and purposes. Raised with you. She only joined the party a month ago." She had managed a harsh whisper that still sounded like yelling.

"I always knew you guys had secret parties. Not cool to not invite me, Lo." My joke fell flat.

"You claim to be my friend, but ever since you became a goblin-witch-soldier-of-fortune, your mind has warped. You'll do anything to win. This isn't a game, Peg. This is my life, and I love him. You're like my sister. You should be happy for me."

"My priorities may have changed, but you're still one of them. Why won't you see reason?" I kept my voice soft. If I spoke any louder, Lola would hear the tears I was holding back and use them against me. Knowing that as a fact, in that moment, hurt more than nearly dying the month before.

Though I thought I hid it well, Lola must have heard because her eyes calmed, and she looked sad. I thought I'd gotten through to her, but then she tensed up again, squaring her shoulders. "We need a break, Peg. I'll call you when…if…I'm ready to talk. Stay away from Michael." Her eyes narrowed in on Vegard. "You too, jackass."

As she walked back to the house, I felt wetness on my cheeks. Did I just lose my best friend? Even worse, would I be able to save her?

9

─────────

Vegard disappeared quickly after Lola did. I didn't blame him because I also didn't know what to do when people cried in front of me. That and we didn't need to discuss anything else. All I wanted when I got home was to bust open a bottle of wine and go to sleep after consuming the whole damn thing. I settled for a Benadryl to prompt sleep that wouldn't come after I completed my chores for the evening, which consisted of preparing all the necessities for the reverse scry spell.

One of my cases had gone completely FUBAR. Of course that would be the job that didn't pay, but Lola's friendship was worth more than a mortgage payment, though gods help me if I didn't make the deadline for Delmy, I'd never let Lola live it down...when she started to talk to me again.

The allergy pill helped me sleep soundly through the night and avoid the normal nightmares that accompanied a hellish day, but the next morning, the hits kept on coming. Deval had agreed to let me come back to his lair to do a reverse scry spell. Normally, I'd be avoiding him right now, but a friendly face seemed nice even if that face didn't want to accidentally commit because his magical storeroom thought we were cute together. So, when I opened my door to find Griselda once again up to the task of chauffeuring a churlish witchlin to a super-secret location, my heart dropped. Fuck them.

It turned out that Deval must have felt at least a little guilty about being a chicken shit because Griselda came equipped with a ridiculously oversized coffee, which made the rejection slightly more bearable. Of course, that could also have been the numbness that was beginning to steal over me. Griselda, to my surprise, actually attempted small talk while driving me with my usual hood. I learned that she had two cats. I guessed that felt like a safe topic after she'd spotted Cheddar. She'd been right, and by the time we landed in the Bat Cave, also known as Deval's super secret lair, my spirits had managed to rise to the level where I at least wasn't contemplating becoming a lone survivalist on some rural mountain range. Anyway, I'd probably just run into another secret goblin lair.

Unmasked in the living room, I set the small duffel I'd brought down on a rug that would probably sell for enough to pay my mortgage for several months. I unzipped the duffel and pulled out three vials, a travel cauldron also known as a small saucepot, a camper stove, and a lighter.

"You're going to be lighting a fire? I'm not sure if Deval would like that," Griselda said from behind my crouched position.

I stood up and waved my arm around the empty room. "Whoopsies, if his majesty can't be bothered to show up, then I don't care if he'd approve. Besides, this is witch magic. I'm a witch, so I know what is necessary."

"Is that so?" Griselda crossed her arms and scowled at me.

"Well, not every witch knows, but in this particular case, I do. I'm not setting a bonfire off in his living room, Griselda. It's a camp stove."

She studied the small one burner contraption as if it were about to go off at any moment.

"Haven't you ever been camping?"

She scowled at me. "Leave me in the wilderness with a pocket knife and return a year later. I would emerge healthy and lead you back to the settlement that I had built in the first month."

I lifted my hands in surrender. "I would be dead or have joined a forest cult if they offered to feed me. This little stove has been in my family for years. My family went on regular camping trips, no survivalist skills here, but my mother would let me use it to make our bacon in the morning. If I were to set anything on fire, I would use every bit of the magic I currently have in my reserve, which wasn't too shabby, to put out said fire. Burning Deval's house down would probably be the straw that led to Deval murdering me and feeding me to the pigs."

"Why would he feed you to the pigs?" Her face scrunched in confusion.

Guess she hadn't seen *Snatch*. "Never mind."

"Since you are the expert here, I will allow it." She went and sat on the sofa, prepared to watch my every move.

"So kind you are, mistress." I gave little bow but turned away before I could see her reaction. Lighting the gas stove, I set the pot on it and cleared my mind. When thoughts of kicking Deval in the balls no longer invaded my mind, I pulled out the three vials and started chanting. Each one contained a mixture to represent the past, present, and future. A dead marigold, a live marigold with roots still attached, and a seed. Mixed in with all three was vodka to purify along with some other herbs that would hold the magic I infused in them for the time being. I doubted my babysitter would be happy about the little boom the alcohol would make, but sometimes magic needed a boom.

Still chanting, I pulled the cork out of vial with the dead marigold representing the past and directed my magic to flow with it into the pot. I leaned back, expecting the small fire surge that left black sparks glittering in the air. A small gasp came from the couch, but Griselda kept her peace. Next, I pulled the cork on vial with the seed representing the future, repeating the process; only this time to emit white sparks. Finally, I pulled the cork on the present because there was no time like the present to find out who our traitor was. The sparks rose, a bright green. Rather than let them disintegrate into the air as I had done with the other two, I pulled them into my energy, bringing with them the ashes of the past and the promise of the future. I directed the spell up into the gold fleck, the perfect conduit and also a brilliant piece of surveillance to hide in a goblin's home.

The magic swirled a tornado of mostly green, glittering with shiny specks of black and white. I directed it, forced it into the bead until every ounce of magic was in there. I stopped chanting and took a step back.

"Is that it?"

"Shhhh."

The magic now released to the universe would follow the original scrying spell, its brother, back to the source. It could be a room over; it could be half a world away. We stayed silent for about five minutes before I heard the tell-tale pop, and the magic whooshed back out of the gold fleck and produced an image. The image was of a spell room. Shelves lined every wall, filled to the brim with books, bottles, jars, and other trinkets. In the middle sat a workstation with a small burner, a padded stool tucked under. *Why do the bad guys get all the sweet digs?*

"Do you recognize it?" I asked.

"No, I hoped you would. It looks to be a witch's place."

"We don't all know each other, Griselda."

"You should. There are few of you left, and there is strength in numbers," she harrumphed.

"Or we're sitting ducks easier to kill in one fell swoop."

She looked chastised. Our numbers really had taken a nosedive in the last few centuries.

"Okay, I know a lot of the witches in town but that doesn't mean we're besties. It takes a lot of trust to allow a magic user into your home, as you well know after all the times you've bundled me to secret locations. So, even if I know the witch, I likely won't recognize that witch's home."

"So, what do we do now?" She gestured at the image before me.

"Now, we get some snacks and wait. This is a live feed. We just need to be patient."

"Have you ever watched the live feed for one of those reality shows where everybody backstabs each other in a house hoping to win a million bucks?" Griselda asked.

"No," I said surprised at her question, as she didn't strike one as the trash TV type.

"Me neither, because it's boring."

"Touché. Don't get too excited at the glamorous life that is being a soldier of fortune."

"I'll try not to," she replied, deadpan. "I'll get us some refreshments. Stay here and do not tell Deval that I left you alone. Also, don't go bonding with another one of his planes."

She had turned to walk out of the room, so she missed the blush that stained my cheeks. *Whoo boy*.

The snacks in the joint, as expected, were top notch. Crispy, but not greasy, tortilla chips with what must have been homemade salsa and an honest to goodness lemon meringue pie. Who had pies just lying around? I didn't. If a pie sat in my kitchen longer than a day, then I hoped somebody had called the coroner because likely the reaper had come for me. She even busted out some diet soda. I doubted that Deval drank the stuff, and she confirmed that she had picked it up for me.

"He advised me to keep you caffeinated. He said you liked sugar in coffee but not in carbonated beverages."

My mouth fell open.

She arched brow at me. "You two are just friends?"

I shoved a bite of pie in my mouth to force it shut. The juxtaposition of sweet and tart hit a note of perfection when combined with the light-as-air meringue. I might forgive him after all.

"Are you eating to avoid questions?"

I swallowed. "Depends, are you asking for yourself or someone else?"

"Myself."

"Well, then I can tell you that I have no idea how to describe our relationship, but at this time, friends is the best description."

"Like that, is it?"

"Between you and me, I don't know how it is. According to a friend, I should just let whatever happens happen."

"That is prudent advice."

"Unfortunately, I don't have a reputation for patience."

"Few people do when it comes to this sort of thing. Of course you seem to do all right sitting around staring at a projection of a room."

"Eh, I can do it if necessary. The sugar and caffeine help, but when it comes to personal matters, that's just not me. I don't like things to stew unless they're in a Crock-Pot."

"You're very food focused."

I shrugged. Truth be told, I was a glutton. "I'm a bona fide member of the clean plate club."

She smiled, scraping the last bite of pie from her plate. "Me, too."

A few days ago, if someone had told me that I'd be sitting with Griselda, eating pie, and gossiping about men, I'd have said that person was insane because Griselda reserved her energies for warrior duties and scowling. Happy to be proved wrong, I ate more pie, not wanting to have to turn in my membership card.

Three hours and some change later, we'd consumed half the pie, half a bag of chips, and what must have been a quart of salsa. I seriously considered unbuttoning my jeans but decided Griselda and I weren't there yet. I'd save my less-than-polite behavior for the future. Little did she know she had that to look forward to, that and me carrying on phone conversations while taking a whiz, the ultimate sign of friendship.

We sat in companionable silence, and my eyes began to flutter. I glanced over at Griselda. Her eyes were alert, staring at the conjuring room projected before us. If I just closed my eyes for a moment, it wouldn't matter. About to give in, I caught some movement in the projection. A woman entered the room. I sat forward, studying her back as she set a tote bag on the workstation. Pulling a few items, she finally turned to face the camera.

"Well, shit." Griselda muttered.

"Yup." I agreed. I rushed forward and began my chant. The projection faded, turning back into a tornado of magic before I pulled the spell back along the line of the original spell. It finally reformed into one ball of spent magic, and I dropped it back into my pot, ready for disposal and turned back to Griselda.

"You want to tell him?"

"That our witch healer has betrayed our people? I don't particularly want to tell him, but it is my duty. Why did you stop the projection? He may have wanted to see it."

"If he did, then he should have shown up today and not just provided snacks. You've witnessed the betrayer, and I don't want her to know we're on to her yet. She'd go into hiding or leave town. Right now, her scrying spell is dormant, but if she decided to pop it open tonight to ogle Deval in his skivvies, she would sense the magic and know that it had been compromised."

"It can be fun when they run." Griselda's grin took on a predatory glint.

I shivered. "Ugh, no thank you. You just reminded me of a certain vampire."

"That was unkind. I may be a skilled tracker, but I'm not a predator."

I threw up my hands. "I know. I know. Right now, I need to clean up, and you need to take me home. There are things that must be done, and you need to go use those tracking skills to deliver some bad news."

She nodded and grabbed the pot to go clean it. I'd

wanted to snoop in Deval's kitchen, but arguing over someone cleaning up for me wasn't something I did. So, I gathered my stuff together, used a little powder room I'm been directed to off the living room, and contemplated my next steps.

A local witch mixed up in treason against the goblins was something Pammy needed to know about. Delmy may have hired me, but it looked like I wouldn't have a choice. Griselda didn't look forward to telling Deval. Well, I really didn't want to get my boss involved, but thems was the breaks.

10

———

The conversation I needed to have with Pammy was not a phone conversation. Once Griselda dropped me off, I quickly fed my cat and headed back out. Anxiety gnawed at my gut. I had no reason to feel guilty. I'd done nothing wrong, but like everyone else, I much preferred to give the man- or woman-, as the case may be, in-charge good news. Instead, I would be telling said woman that a member of her coven who had secretly been working for the goblins also had secretly betrayed said goblins. The political machinations involved made my head hurt.

In fact, by the time my Jeep rumbled into the strip mall that held Pammy's unofficial headquarters, Bump and Grind, I'd begun to feel some sharp shooting pain behind my eyes. More caffeine, the usual answer to my problems, was helpfully served at this establishment. I walked in and waved to Pammy, currently holding court in her corner, the best seats in the house. She occupied an entire sofa; her curvy but muscular frame sprawled in the center. As usual, none of her minions dared sit by her, instead taking the wingback chairs that had been dragged around a solid, if well worn, coffee table at the center.

She arched a brow at me, and I pointed to the counter and then back to her. She nodded, understanding more poor mime work. A hot dirty chai with an extra espresso shot for good measure held with reverence in my hands, I walked confidently over to Pammy. Well...I didn't drag my feet.

The courtiers had been shooed to other corners of the room. I didn't visit to socialize, and she'd gotten in the habit of dismissing her people before I approached. I appreciated this mainly because the truly devoted did not like being shooed, and I didn't like being on the receiving end of stink eye from people I did not know. A wingback chair sat closest to Pammy and also happened to be my favorite, so I plopped into it, set my purse on the table, and took a sip of the too hot chai.

"Well, you're about to deliver shit news," Pammy muttered.

"Why do you think that?" I asked gingerly, as my mouth had just been scalded in the attempt to put off the conversation for five more seconds.

"You burnt your tongue, didn't you?"

I nodded.

"Personal injury to avoid telling me something, you're not the first, and you won't be the last. Tell Pammy your troubles."

"The last time you said that, I ended up with alcohol poisoning and taking a job I was clearly unqualified for."

"No one starts out qualified. Now look at you kicking ass and taking names."

"I'm glad you think so. There's a problem."

"There's a million problems constantly compounding,

so what is this one?" Pammy waved her hand, urging me to move it along.

"You know how the goblins use a witch healer?"

"Yep, even know who she is, even though she pretends like it's some big secret."

Not surprising. "Well, the not-so-secret healer has betrayed them."

Pammy abandoned her easy pose and sat forward, her elbows on her knees. A few of the dreads that she currently sported wrapped up in a bun had escaped and fell forward, their whimsical presence a contradiction to the hardness of her eyes. "Don't leave out any details."

I told her the whole thing. Scrying, reverse scryings, treasonous witch healers, and all. Pammy leaned back once I'd finished. The chai latte now lukewarm, I guzzled it anyway.

"Go get a to-go drink."

"Why?"

"We're going on a bust. I'm gonna nip this shit in the bud before Delmy finds out."

"She may have already," I pointed out.

"Yep, but it's still my job. The healer will be punished, but she's a witch. Despite her employment choices, she's mine. Only by my will."

"How very regal of you."

"I wish it were that easy. I maintain my position only by the choice of the witches and because of that a strong reaction is necessary."

Not the best time to point out that Pammy would only go down when she chose to or in a combustion of magical forces, so I listened to her advice and got another drink for the road. She drove us because she knew where Millicent, the healer, lived and being a passenger would no doubt contradict her control-freak ways. In recent days,

I'd become used to being a hooded passenger and being able to look out the window a novelty that I found I enjoyed. We got on the 60 and headed east. Truth be told, there wasn't much to see beyond the same generic southwest-type designs on the block walls surrounding the freeway and some half-hearted xeriscaping, but I could see!

Pammy didn't talk for the first fifteen minutes, probably contemplating what she planned to do or maybe that she should make banana bread from some overripe fruit. I didn't know since I was definitely not the Pammy whisperer, though if what Griselda said about me being an heir apparent was true, I might want to learn the language to steer Pammy off of that particular course.

"You know your role in this?" Pammy glanced over at me.

"General lackey extraordinaire?"

"Good girl." Her eyes returned to the road.

Eh, I'd meant that as a joke. "What does being a lackey generally entail in your mind?" I asked.

"You stand to my side, a little behind. You have your magic primed and ready to go, not aimed at my back preferably."

"So, that's why I'm to the side," I snarked.

"Smart ass."

"Yup, so is this a be seen-not-heard kinda gig?"

"I said you were smart."

"But you also added the word 'ass.'"

Pammy turned her stone cold gaze on me. "Appropriate, I would say."

I shrugged and only began to sweat a little, not at her stare, but at the fact that I strongly believed in keeping one's eyes on the road. She eventually glanced away from me, making a sharp exit that had another driver honking and displaying a finger known for its vulgarity. Pammy returned the gesture and continued on her way.

Millicent lived in an older neighborhood that mainly consisted of brown on brown. Brown bricks with desert landscaping in the seventies-style ranch homes. The neighborhood boasted large yards with rocks for easy maintenance plus some stellar views of the Superstition Mountains.

The car stopped; I got out and began to walk up the driveway of the house we parked in front of.

"Where you going?"

I stopped. "To see Millicent?"

"That's not her house."

"Then why did we park in front of it?"

"To be stealthy."

I looked at her and gestured toward a general entrance area. "We're literally walking up to the front door."

"Yep."

"That's not the definition of stealth."

She rolled her eyes. "Get behind me, minion."

"And slightly to the side."

She ignored that and walked down the sidewalk. We walked to a house three lots down. We approached the front door and rang the bell. Waiting on the porch, super stealthily. A dog barked, but the sound came from a neighbor's yard, and a few moments later, we heard some rustling before the front door opened.

"Hello, Millicent." Pammy's voice came out dark and foreboding.

The door sported a security screen, so I couldn't quite see the woman, but she remained silent.

"Open the door, Millicent."

The pause only lasted a few seconds before the sound of the deadbolt turning hit my ears and the door opened.

The small red head stood frozen in her entryway. Obviously planning to bum around for the day, she wore yoga pants and long-sleeve thermal shirt. She began to twist the hem of said shirt.

"I didn't expect you, Pammy."

"That's the point. Won't you be so kind to invite us in? I'm parched from the drive. You've met my associate."

So focused on Pammy's imposing figure, she seemed to notice me for the first time and gave me a shaky nod. "Please, come in."

She stood back, but Pammy gestured for Millicent to keep moving, not wanting the woman at her back. We came to a large sunken living room common in these types of homes. Two overstuffed leather couches with some heavy wood tables framed an extra-large television on the wall. Pammy took her seat. A seat that looked suspiciously more worn than the other seats in the room. Damn, the woman had just taken Millicent's seat in her own home. Like the good minion that I currently played, I stood behind her and a little to the left, the front door behind me.

"I'd love an iced tea if you have one. Preferably unsweetened, but I can do sweet."

"Sun tea?" Millicent asked, referring to the Arizona habit of leaving glass jars of water outdoors with tea bags in them to let nature do the work. The sunshine managed this despite the cooler winter temperatures, a benefit of desert life.

"That will be fine."

"Peg?"

"I'm fine." I wanted the damn tea but that wasn't my role today.

"Don't go thinking about sneaking out the back, Millicent," Pammy called out when the other woman had turned. "We need to talk, and I'm your best bet at getting out of this mess with your hide intact."

"I haven't done anything," came a shaky response from the other room.

"Girl, lying to me ain't gonna help you. You can go around healing for whoever you damn well please. I myself appreciate people who find creative ways to earn a living. Goblin payroll? Good, take their gold, but, young lady, we do not double dip. People who double dip end up dead or with mono, and you got mono, you wish you were dead."

"Always the colorful analogies," I muttered. I knew for a fact that Pammy laid it on whenever she was stressed.

She glared back at me but turned forward as Millicent returned with the requested tea in hand. "You put anything in this?"

"Ice." She trembled slightly.

"Great, another smart ass."

Millicent glanced at me briefly and took a seat on the sofa across from us.

"So, question really is why on earth would a healer do something to hurt a cush job that paid well, had a little air of mystery to it, and paid holidays."

"I don't have paid holidays," Millicent answered the rhetorical question.

I couldn't see Pammy's face from my vantage, but I was pretty sure she rolled had her eyes.

"Not my point. What stupid thing has you spying on the goblin prince that employs you?"

"Did you tell her?" She looked up at me, accusation in her tone.

"Nobody needs to tell me you've been working for the goblins. You've been at it for two years. I am the sheriff. Of course I knew, but it was a good job for you, even if they wanted to keep it quiet. It also brought a level of goodwill, a tie between our two communities, which you have royally fucked. Question still remains, why?"

"There's no why." She looked at the floor.

"Honey, there is always a why. I'm hoping this time around it's because some big bad threatened you. I can work with that. Better not be that you wanted some extra cash to buy the super deluxe television you got hanging on your wall."

Millicent looked up, and I saw the hope in her eyes at a possible savior. Ding, ding, ding, big bad for the winner.

"I didn't need money. The goblins pay more than a fair price. I needed to stay alive."

Pammy nodded. "You should have come to me."

"I couldn't."

"Yes, you could. There is nothing out there that scares me. Even if it did, I would still defend you. It is my duty and my privilege."

Wow, I'd always thought of Pammy as a power-hungry mover and shaker. The realization that, beyond the political acrobats and the adoring masses, she genuinely wanted to protect and serve us was humbling.

"I was scared."

"When you're scared in the future you come to me, capisce?"

Her lower lip trembled, and tears formed in her eyes, but she nodded raising her hand to hastily wipe a few tears that escaped her eyes.

"Okay then, time to tell me what has you going and setting scrying spells on the goblin monarchy."

She hesitated, staring at the floor. After about thirty tense seconds she took a deep breath and looked up at Pammy. "There's a witch family that comes to town every so often. They have so much power, but it's all tainted. When I was a child I saw them do—things," she hesitated.

"Things?"

"My family didn't have a lot of money. We lived in a trailer park."

"Nothing wrong with a manufactured home," Pammy interjected at the woman's hesitation.

"I know that, but there was a lot of turnover in the tenants, but one family came back summer after summer. I was so happy that there were other witches in the neighborhood. Normally it was just me, my mom, and one other witch family in the park, the family of my best friend, Julia. The other neighbors weren't always nice when they realized we were witches. But whenever this family came, the other people left us alone. The humans were afraid of them. Julia and I used to go over and play at their house when our moms were working. There was something off about them, but they were so nice. They kept the awful people away from us, and they always had these butter cookies. We loved it there.

"One night my mom was working her second job. I went over to Julia's to play. I opened the door. We used to just walk into each other's homes. The matriarch was leaning over Julia's mom, and her son was over Julia. The rest of the family encircled them. I could see the magic: they were feeding on them somehow. I wanted to help them, but I was ten and scared. I ran."

"You did the right thing, hon. Nothing you could have done to help them."

She inhaled sharply. "I know that logically, but part of me still wonders if I could have saved them."

"Look at me." Pammy leaned forward.

Millicent's head snapped up to meet Pammy's eyes.

"If you could see the feeding magic, and they were in the circle, it was too late. Let's say you managed to stop an entire family coven of drainers. Only, the shells that would have been left would have been insane shadows of their former selves. Not mental illness, fixed-with-medication-and-therapy insane, constantly screaming, hurting themselves and others, terrified, life-as-a-constant-nightmare insane. A living horror film."

"How can you possibly know that?" Millicent asked.

"I've been around. You think they let just anyone be sheriff?"

"The rule of might," I mumbled.

Pammy snapped her head back and gave me a hard look. "Might helps, but the masses outnumber the leader. Might, intelligence, compassion, that is what brings the goodwill of the people, along with a few heroic deeds." She turned away from me then, back to being focused on Millicent, and I decided to keep my mouth shut for the rest of this visit.

"What happened next?"

"I ran and got the bike my mom had bought me at a yard sale. I raced to the motel on Main Street where my mom cleaned, and I found her. I told her what I saw. She took me to the front office. The night manager was out smoking in the parking lot. She cleared out the safe, grabbed her purse, put me in our beat-up station wagon, and drove all night to get to my grandma's house in Colorado. We only stopped once to get gas and for her to use a payphone. I don't know who she called, but I lived in Colorado until I moved back here five years ago."

"She called me," Pammy said.

"What?" She tilted her head to the side, her face scrunching up.

"She left a rambling message about drainers but didn't say who she was. Just that it happened at Sunshine RV Living. I went there, but I couldn't find any witches. You're right about your neighbors. Those particular sets of humans were assholes."

"That sounds like my mom. She wasn't a fighter, but I'm glad she called you."

"Me, too, though I wished she had called me again. So, this was what, twenty years ago? When did they come back?"

"A year ago. The son found me. He'd aged. He'd been just a child when he killed Julia, or at least I thought he was. I didn't even recognize him, but he came here. Knocked on my door, told me what he wanted, and that if I didn't do that he'd kill me like he had my friend."

"Have you seen him since?"

"No, he zapped me with some sort of sleeping spell. When I came to, I was in my bed. I thought I'd dreamed the whole thing until I looked at my nightstand. He'd written instructions to what he'd wanted done along with instructions to burn the note once I'd completed my task, so they'd know...there was also a butter cookie sitting there. I did what he said."

"Do you remember what the name of the family was?"

"The Mc—" Millicent's head snapped back, her body going taut as her mouth opened to emit an ear-piercing scream of pain and terror. Black magic poured out of her mouth circling her body.

I started around the couch, but Pammy stood and held her hand out. "It's too late. We are leaving right now."

"What do you mean it's too late?" I asked, incredulous. I started toward Millicent.

"Margaret Elizabeth Darrow—walk out of the door."

The shock at being triple-named along with the slight compulsion in her voice had me adjusting course and jogging to the door. When I opened it, Pammy was right behind me. I looked over her shoulder to Millicent. The magic was gone. All that was left was a body blackened, her eyes opened in fear and torment. Pammy pushed me forward.

"We need to go now."

Millicent was beyond help, but I still hesitated.

"That spell has a contagious property. We need to go now if we have any hope of being alive in the next hour." We sprinted to the car.

11

P ammy drove as though our lives depended upon it, not even bothering to return the honks, vulgar hand gestures, or profanities screamed out windows as she drove with reckless abandon.

"I think I'm fine, Pammy. I don't feel bad at all," I said, trying to get her to drive more safely.

"You think Millicent felt bad? She had that spell riding in her blood for a year. In exactly one hour we will be blackened corpses if we don't take countermeasures. It's a sneaky spell meant to kill anyone who triggers it, and the people surrounding them. Take out the snitch; take out the witnesses."

Fear, icy and sudden, sent a shiver up my spine and numbed my hands. I didn't speak after that. Pammy needed to drive, and she had barely avoided about three accidents in the ten minutes that we'd been in the car.

We pulled up to her house, a patio home in Tempe, twenty minutes later. We got out of the car and walked briskly to the front door. When she opened it and went inside, I hesitated. She'd never invited me in her home before, always conducting our business on her back patio if necessary.

"Get your ass in here."

I obeyed and followed her. Normally I'd have taken the time to study her home, but I barely noticed that she owned furniture as I followed her to the back of the house. Pammy had a spell room set up in a den area. White cabinets lined one wall with different symbols painted on each. When she reached to open the one that had a black skull appearing to laugh manically on it, I began to shiver violently. I still felt fine, but considering the other cabinets had flowers, animals, and runes painted on them, this cabinet further reinforced the danger we were in.

The cabinet contained row after row of test tubes in holders, all corked and neatly labeled. She got out a step-stool and climbed it, reaching a hand to the top shelf. She strained, grasping for something that had been pushed to the back. A grunt of success escaped her as she pulled out two vials. She climbed down and handed one to me, the liquid in it a thick and inky black.

Pammy pulled out her cork. "Quit studying it. You need to drink it."

I pulled out my cork and Pammy startled me by clinking her vial to mine. "May we live long and prosper, oh, and murder our enemies."

I'd drink to that. "Amen."

We drank. The liquid was gritty and bitter, but I held my head back, swallowed every drop, and considered licking the tube for good measure. My body seized up. I lost all control and fell to the floor. My heart stopped, and my vision blackened. I felt no pain when my body hit the floor, and for a brief moment, I hovered over myself. Just as quickly, I was sucked back into my body. My chest throbbed as my heart began again and lungs seized in a death gasp. Across from me, Pammy made a similar noise. I stared at her. We both were sprawled on our sides, breathing as if we'd just learned how. After a few minutes, our breathing steadied.

"What did you just have me take?" I asked. My voice sounded faded to my own ears.

"Reaper."

"What?" I yelled. Well, more likely said in a very hoarse but firm tone.

Reaper was a last-ditch potion, meant for the foolish or the desperate. Mostly the desperate. When a powerful spell locked on you and there was no cure, your only option to remove it was death. Reaper killed you, hopefully for only the moment it would take the spell to abandon a corpse, but you didn't always wake up. Last I'd heard, your chances were sixty-forty to begin with and went down by about ten percent with each dose.

"No choice. We were already dead."

I lay there. I knew I should get up, but shock at the severity of our situation hit me.

"On the bright side, you'll have earned some serious street cred for this," Pammy said, trying to lighten the mood.

"For standing too close when a magical plague went off, taking a potion that I didn't even think to ask what it was, or surviving Reaper?"

"We need to teach you how to spin a tale. You heroically tried to save a woman who was already in her death throes, risked the world's most dangerous cure, so you could come back from the brink of death to avenge a fellow witch."

"I'll be sure to tell my mom that version."

"She'll be worried, but happy that you're on a serial killer case."

I sat up, my body willing to move now that the shock had worn off. "You're right." My mother loved any story crime-related, serial killing being the ultimate crime. "But how did you know that?"

"Peg, I know every witch in this state. I have spoken with each and every one of them. It's my job."

"And your privilege."

"Caught that, did you?"

"Yep, I didn't realize that you cared that much."

She sat up, looking flabbergasted. "Of course, I care. Yes, it's nice to be the boss, but I would not willingly put up with this headache if I didn't believe that I could help, to improve our lives, to make a better world for the next generation."

"I don't even know if that's possible for witches. The fear runs too deep." I hadn't even realized my own cynical view until I said the words out loud.

Pammy looked at me. Most of the time her face was hard, authoritative, or filled with laughter. This was the first time I'd seen genuine sadness. "Hope is important, Peg. We will find a way. If we don't, our children will."

We stood up gingerly. My shoulder ached, probably from the unexpected tumble. Pammy tested her body from side to side, her hands on her hips. Her spine cracked audibly. I winced.

She caught my facial expression. "The body creaks as you get older."

"What? I thought you were immortal?"

"Not now, maybe someday–hope, remember?"

"I'm not even sure I'd want to be immortal if I had the opportunity."

"Your psyche yearns for what is lost, but you've

accepted your untimely demise. Given the opportunity, you'd take the thousand years that were supposed to be ours, even if only to keep the hussies off of your goblin boy toy."

"Seriously, Pammy, where do you get all this information?" I glared at her.

"None of your business. Besides, I know a lot of things, but I wasn't certain about that until you just confirmed it. If you don't want people to think you have something going on, you shouldn't look at them like they're chocolate cake at holiday parties."

"He was there with another woman. Why wouldn't you just think I was admiring an attractive man?"

"Your reaction to the other woman. You didn't cause a scene or try to pull her hair out. Really, I was rather impressed. Proved to me that you were maturing."

"I would never do that. It's not her fault if he asked her out."

"That right there. Levelheaded. I can appreciate that. Truth be told, I would have caused a scene in my youth. Tables woulda been flipped and hair snatched, but time mellows, and we eventually get to the same levelheaded conclusion you have managed at such a youthful age. Of course there's nothing wrong with a little passion."

"You make me sound boring."

"Under that fine layer of reserve, you're not boring. What I'm telling you is that a youthful scene can be overlooked. So, if you're going to let go and live a little, pull a little hair, now is the time to do it."

"I'll take it under advisement."

"See that you do. We need to go back to Millicent's."

"I know." I agreed, my stomach flipping at the thought of seeing the blackened corpse of a woman who had been a vibrant living being a few hours ago.

"The body is gone."

"Wha—" I stood on my toes to try to look past Pammy. I topped her by a few inches, but she had stepped onto the entrance to the house, making it difficult to see beyond her. Sure enough past the entryway. I had a clear line of sight to where Millicent's body had lain a few hours ago.

"Whoever set the trigger must have been alerted. We're going in, but I need you on your toes, primed and ready. If there are any surprises, you zap first and ask questions later."

I nodded and followed Pammy into the house. Quietly, we worked to clear the house. Not a living or dead soul occupied the house other than us. To make matters worse, the home had been scrubbed magically. It was as though nothing had occurred in the house. Once the scrub spell faded, the house wouldn't show any recent magic. Any witches who came into the house wouldn't even be able to tell that another witch had lived here unless they happened to go into her or his spell-working room.

We finished our search by looking in the backyard. Nothing to note except for some well-placed lawn furniture and more xeriscaping. Standing there in the yard, we both looked around. At that point even some out-of-place gravel would have been an exciting clue, but it all sat neatly in the yard.

"What are we going to do now?"

"We are going to have a meet with the goblins."

Huh? I turned to look at her. "I thought this was a witch matter." I mimicked the exact wording she'd used million times before.

"You thought wrong. Looks like your paid gig and your personal one have collided. Millicent was about to say the name McAllisters. The goblins need to know. These creatures are more dangerous than vampires."

"You can't mean that," I said.

"Vampires are born without consciences. It's not actually their fault that they're psychopaths. These witches use the darkest of magics, with skill and finesse, and even more frightening than that, they use their dark magic with joy. Nothing is more dangerous than that type of creature."

I managed to close my mouth and nodded. "I guess that makes sense."

"Damn right, it makes sense. You need to learn to trust experience."

"My own as well? Because the experiences I've had with the vampires makes me reluctant to put something above them on the beings-of-darkness scale."

Pammy glowered at me.

"No, I know what you're saying, and I hear you. My family just has a particularly dark history with the vampires," I said, referring to my aunt who had become a thrall and blood slave to the vampires for a period of time before escaping. She still suffered from what she had endured.

"Your family has survived a lot, and I know it isn't over yet, but let's focus on one twisted asshole at a time. You want to call to set up the meet, or do you want me to?"

I thought about it for a moment. "I have the personal connection, as you pointed out, though it's not as serious as you would assume. I think you'd better do it. When you call, they know we mean business. They'd still come if I called, but I think it's better if you do."

"Now you're learning."

I hadn't realized that I'd just been given a test, but before I could make some surly reply, Pammy had her phone out and was dialing. I leaned in. I didn't want to miss a word.

"Pammy here. Please tell Delmy I need to speak with her," then she hung up the phone.

My mouth opened and closed as I just stared at Pammy. I pointed at the phone. "Did you just hang up on the goblin queen?"

She swatted my hand away. "No, just her secretary. Delmy will call back."

"And if she doesn't?"

Pammy rolled her eyes. "Do you think this is the first conversation that I've had with Delmy? She knows I mean no disrespect, and she will call as soon as she's able. Even the secretary knows I don't like to be put on hold. It's either bullshit elevator music or silence all the while I'm wishing I could be playing solitaire on my phone rather than sitting here staring into space."

The phone rang, causing me to jump and proving Pammy's point.

"Delmy, I hope you're well. Thank you, I am also in good health. We seem to have a mutual problem. Are you available for a meet? Tomorrow morning will be fine. Deval is a suitable substitute. Peg Darrow will also be joining us since our mutual problem is in relation to the job you hired her for. Health to you and your family."

I wished I had enhanced hearing, so I could hear the formal muckity-muck from both ends. It just about warmed my peon heart.

"We're set for tomorrow." Pammy said, returning her phone to her pocket and turning back to me. "Go home, charge yourself, and feed your cat. Try calling that friend of yours."

"Uh, Lola is not really answering my calls right now."

"Try anyway. If she's under their thumb, magical or

otherwise, I want her to know she has help when the shit eventually hits the fan. I will speak with the goblins about a possible extraction, but I'm not sure if that will be possible because free will is important. Your friend needs to make her choices on her own."

"Even if those stupid choices end up killing her?"

"I didn't say that, but forcing her out against her will may cause her more harm than good. You saw what happened to Millicent. Our best bet would be to kill that nest of vipers. Anything they may have done to her will likely fade with their death, and even if not, it would be a hell of a lot easier to remove any dark curse they may have placed on her without constantly worrying about someone setting whatever it may be off."

I'd let the hurt I'd felt at Lola's rejection hide the extent of the danger she was in under a wall of antipathy. Tears began to form in my eyes when reality finally hit me. I knew she'd been in danger, but I hadn't been willing to acknowledge it. I tilted my head back and let out a sniffle.

"None of that now. I know you were ostriching the worst of it, but you will do everything in your power to help her. Put aside the rejection and remember the girl who would walk into a vampire den with you. She's still there. She's just confused. Life hasn't been easy on Lola, and a friend from her former life, the life where her parents were alive, is a hard thing to shake off. Deep down she knows something is wrong, and she'll protect herself when the time comes. Or I will. Or you will."

I sniffed again getting my emotions under control. Shockingly enough, in the past I rarely cried, but the last few weeks had been a big adjustment, and the shit storm wouldn't seem to stop. A shiver ran through my body. I was at a point where I could walk away from all of this. I might not be able to get job as a teacher due to discrimination, but I could get some menial job. A hard day's work was satisfying, whether it was scrubbing toilets or fighting off serial killers, but I wasn't ready to admit defeat, and the way Pammy looked at me right now, like I had something to offer, had me squaring my shoulders, ready to save Lola and kill some drainers.

12

Pammy sent me home to get some sleep, though the fact that she'd also bought me a large latte for the road suggested she didn't really think I'd be getting much, or she realized the extent of my caffeine tolerance because I slept like a baby. The numbers on my clock even indicated that I'd managed a full eight. Not too shocking when I noticed the soft lavender glow of magic surrounding my bed. George had apparently thought I needed rest.

I'd called Lola about a dozen times, leaving voicemails that ranged from angry to cajoling, and even included me making up a song about Cheddar for her enjoyment, though the ditty may have actually dissuaded her. But no, the girl I knew would enjoy a jaunty tune about a large orange cat that ate a wheel of cheese for daring to have the same name as him. I checked my phone when I woke up from my assisted slumber. Not a peep.

Defeat on that front, I showered and dressed. A pair of dark slim-fit jeans with enough elastic in them to be form fitting without making me constantly wonder when I could trade them out for yoga pants, a burnt-orange sweater, and flat ankle boots made up my ensemble. My hair blow dried into a large halo of curls and makeup applied, I felt a brief moment of control. When everything was wrong, dressing like you meant business helped. At least it did for me.

The meet was scheduled for nine a.m. at Bump and Grind. I'd begun to suspect Pammy was at least a partial owner of the establishment. I don't know why that hadn't occurred to me before. At the very minimum, the woman paid their electric bill. I arrived fifteen minutes early. Pammy was in her usual spot. Her people had already been relocated to a table across the room. I waved at them. Startled, only two waved back. I'd been dismissive of them in the past, thinking they were just groupies and boot lickers. Maybe they were, but they were witches, and frankly I'd started to realize why they flocked to the woman currently sitting of a sofa sipping a frothy concoction. She'd earned our respect.

I purchased another frothy concoction for myself and went to join her. Normally I'd leave her with the couch to herself, but she scooted over. The only time she'd ever had me sit with her was during a meet with the vampires. Apparently during inter-species meetings, we sat together. I liked it.

"Dorothy," she called out and gestured to a middle-aged woman who sat at the table, one of the women who'd waved back. She quickly walked over. Sitting, the joiner looked rather harmless in a faded floral button up, her graying black hair in a French twist. As she had walked over, I noticed her stride. She walked confidently, with a purpose. Her stance was remarkably similar Griselda's as a matter of fact.

"Dorothy, Peg, Peg, Dorothy." Pammy introduced us.

"Nice to meet you." I stood up from my place of honor and shook her hand.

"Likewise, I've seen you around."

I nodded. I had seen her, but just not really seen her until now.

"Dorothy is also a fortune. I asked her to come today."

I smiled. "With this group, the more the merrier."

"Can't blame you there. I'm semi-retired, but when Pammy said there were drainers in town, I knew I couldn't sit this one out." She'd lowered her voice at the word drainers. No need to cause a panic and all that.

Before we could delve further into the situation, Deval walked in. A hush fell over the room, or maybe that was just in my head as the blood rushed to my ears. He'd decided formal as well, even if his formal was a fitted gray suit and mine was a sweater instead of a T-shirt and closed-toe shoes. He strode over to us, his eyes resting on mine for a moment before turning to Pammy. The small spark of heat in my stomach quickly cooled when I remembered his earlier behavior. I planted what I hoped was a professional facade on my face and took my seat next to Pammy.

"Ladies, thank you for the invitation. It's a privilege." He nodded at each of us in turn.

"Please sit, Deval." Pammy gestured to the wingback chair that had been set across from the sofa.

"My mother mentioned that the affair we hired Peg for has taken an unexpected turn."

"That's one way to put it," I muttered.

Pammy held her hand up, silencing me. "It appears that the family that blackmailed Millicent into setting the scrying spell is also a family responsible for unspeakable acts against the witches. They are also the ones who set magic against your cousin."

"What are the witches doing to remedy this problem?"

Deval asked, the personal side I had begun to know hidden firmly behind a stoic mask.

"We will take care of our own problems," Pammy snapped, clearly annoyed at the implication.

"I am not saying you are unaided, Pammy. My mother expressly advised me to offer any assistance we can, but since this is a witch matter, there are limits to what we are able to do, as you well know from the mutual agreements we have in place. We have no wish for any altercations."

"Well, then, let me make myself clear with two witnesses present."

"Two witch witnesses."

"Really, Deval?" Pammy asked glancing briefly at me.

My mouth dropped, but I shut it quickly. Deval gave me a hard stare. I glared right back at him. He inclined his head slightly, which I took to be the question as to whether I'd told Pammy about my goblin heritage. I rolled my eyes in return, which he apparently took as a "no" because he refocused on Pammy.

"She is still yours."

"She is, but as you've gotten to know her; you should know she wouldn't betray any agreements. It would not be wise for the witches to go to war, Deval."

"I'm surprised you would admit as much."

I'd held my tongue too long. "Quit being such a pompous jackass. Nobody wants war. She said it wouldn't be wise, not that we wouldn't do it."

"Thank you, Margaret," Pammy said with a dry tone.

"Yes, Pamela." I responded curtly. See how she enjoyed the full name schtick.

She took a moment to turn, giving me one hard look, making me swallow, before returning her gaze to Deval. "Back to my associate's appropriately phrased 'pompous' remarks. My witches are ready and able to go to war, but war would be foolish. Weakening both of our families and opening the way for the vampires to come and usurp both of our seats. Yes, other states would eventually come to reclaim the land, but not before we'd all been used as a buffet. So, whereas I know you're posturing, we both know you and your mother want war even less. Now stop goading, Peg."

"What do I have to do with him being an ass?" Apparently my diplomacy skills were waning.

"Good lord, woman, exactly what I meant. Dorothy, have I not had dozens of these types of meetings with Deval sitting in for his mother over the years?"

"Yes, Pammy."

"Have you ever seen Deval act quite this antagonistic?"

"No, he's usually pretty charming. Even funny occasionally."

"So, what I mean, Peg, is I think you two have unresolved issues because although he knows that witnesses usually remain quiet unless asked a question, and you know that, he decided to get under your skin. You fell for it, and we'll need to work on that."

I felt my cheeks heat but kept my mouth shut. My only joy was that Deval, too, looked chastised.

"I'm not going to verify your accusations, Pammy. Let's get back to the business at hand," Deval said in a more casual tone. "Please tell me more about this family and how you believe that the goblins might be of assistance."

"The McAllisters are a witch family we believe to be drainers and general practitioners of the darker sides of magic."

"Yes, I would also classify draining to be on the darker side," he deadpanned.

Pammy ignored him and continued with explaining their history in Arizona, their whispered reputation through other regions of the U.S., along with Millicent's recount of her traumatic childhood experience and the threats used to make her betray him. Once she finished, we all sat in silence for a moment.

"It saddens me that Millicent did not come to either of our houses. I would have gladly protected her, as I know you would have."

Pammy nodded. "I would have done everything in my power to do so. Sadly, I realize now that it would have been too late for her. The curse set to her was instantaneous. I've only witnessed it one other time in my lifetime as a child. Had I not, both Peg and I would have also fallen victim to these monsters."

He sat forward in the chair looking between Pammy and me. "I'm sorry I hadn't realized that harm had come to either of you."

"Yep, as a survivor of Reaper, I bet I can even raise my rates," I cut in.

I expected a chastisement from Pammy at interrupting yet again, but instead I got a full belly laugh. "That's my girl. Damn right, we'll raise your rates."

"I don't see how this is funny." Deval studied me.

"She's fine Deval, and you're right, getting the blow-back from a death curse isn't funny, but profiting from taking a potion that guarantees a certain death for a small while to circumvent a permanent one and then getting paid extra for a necessity because it offers the illusion that you're a hard ass is hilarious."

I leaned forward and looked over at Dorothy, who'd remained quiet this whole time. "Please don't mention to anyone that I'm more of a self preservationist than a hard ass."

She didn't speak, but she did grin before closing her mouth, miming zipping it and locking it.

"Ladies, we've gotten off track again. Pardon me, I'm going to go and get a coffee while you compose yourselves." He stood abruptly, his stride sharp as he marched over to the counter.

"He certainly has a bee in his bonnet," Dorothy commented now that we were alone.

"Boy's upset. He didn't protect his healer, and now his girl is out gallivanting around getting herself killed. It's not a comfortable place for him."

"I'm not his girl," I felt the need to point out.

"That's to be decided, but even if you're not 'his girl,' you're a friend, and that's just as bad. We all want to protect our friends."

Lola flashed in my mind. I pulled my phone out to send her a quick text, asking her to call me again.

Pammy gave me a questioning look.

I shook my head negative.

She sighed. "I've changed my mind about Lola. We may need to do an extraction, willing or not. I assumed she would keep at least a minimum amount of contact with you."

"Nope, she's been ignoring me all together."

"That is concerning," Deval sat down, holding a mug that looked like regular ol' black coffee. "Are her foster parents aware that she's involved with this family?"

"We haven't made any notifications because she is an adult. Plus, we don't have many connections in your community, Peg excluded of course. We'd hoped that she would come to her senses, but it's gotten serious. Is she still going to work?"

Deval took out his sleek phone and dialed out. "Good morning, I had hoped to speak with Miss Fahl, is she in today? On vacation? How lovely. How much of this vacation has she taken? All right then, I'll stop by in a week."

He hit "end" on his phone. "She's using some vacation time to get away. Apparently, she's had some stockpiled for a while now."

"That is unfortunate. Please check with her family to see if she's been in touch."

"You don't want to flat out tell them? They could likely lure her away."

"I have no doubt that Lola would respond to her adopted mother's request, but after what happened with Millicent, I believe an extraction would best be done by myself or Alice, who is unfortunately on a road trip at the moment, evading vampires." Deval went to interrupt but Pammy placed her hand up. She had no qualms shushing anyone. "That, young man, is a story for another day."

"You do realize that I'm older than you are, right?"

"No shit? I really must know what moisturizer you use," Pammy snapped. "Now, given that you've brought up your age, and I'm guessing that you were asked for input when deciding about adopting Lola into your fold, I'm going to ask you to think back. The McAllisters were around just prior to her parents' deaths. In that time, do you recall if there were any odd comings and goings with strange witch families and your family? There has to be a connection."

"Why would you say there has to be a connection?"

"I really doubt the family had Millicent set a scrying spell exclusively for them. They would have found no value in stealing your *chest*," she empathized. "Unless, of course, they either had a buyer or they were assisting the actual persons responsible."

"That is logical. Give me moment." He sat back in his chair with his eyes closed.

We sat in silence for several minutes. I used those minutes to drink my latte, becoming more antsy the closer to the bottom of the cup I came. I went to stand to get another, but Pammy grabbed my hand and gave me a hard stare. So, that was a "no" on the refill.

I looked at Deval, whose eyes were now open, looking at our interaction with amusement. "Let her get another drink, Pammy. Reaper won't kill her, but surely caffeine deprivation will."

My cheeks heated but not enough to stop me from standing. "Anyone else want another?"

"Yep, and you're buying," Pammy accepted ungraciously.

Turned out everyone did, so I was twenty dollars poorer. *Worth it.* After handing out the assorted tray the barista provided, I grabbed my latte and listened. It had turned out Deval's meditative state had jarred loose an old memory.

"Two decades ago, Gregar did have a friendship with a young blond man whom I believed to be a witch. In centuries past, this would not have been that odd, but, as you know, our kind have drifted apart in recent years. So, it was unusual."

"Did you ever meet this witch personally or ask Gregar about him."

"As I'm sure you know, my cousin and I are not close. The only reason I knew about it is that I remember going to dinner one night and Gregar happened to be at the bar with said witch. I went to say hello, and when introduced, the twit couldn't resist zapping me like a juvenile; otherwise, I'd have never even known his heritage."

"Do you remember the name he gave you?"

"I do not. I asked Gregar about him at a formal dinner soon after that. I believe he told me to mind my own business or something along those lines. I, of course, mentioned that an unknown witch fraternizing with my cousin was my business."

"Let me guess: that got you the middle finger?" Pammy asked drily.

Deval inclined his head. "I'm sure that was his desired response; however, there is still an illusion of respect shown. He simply said that the witch's family were travelers and would soon move on, so not to worry myself. I should have followed up on it, but, frankly, it was a busy time. Relations weren't quite as hostile, so I took his word for it."

"Blond, cocky witch with a family that moves frequently. Sounds like our guy," Pammy said.

I hesitated but cut in to the conversation yet again. "It sounds like him, Pammy, but Michael was Lola's childhood friend, not a grown adult twenty years ago."

Deval and Pammy looked at each other for a moment before he began to speak. "If my memory serves me, I do recall learning a bit about drainers during my studies. Life sources can be stolen to return youth to whatever point you wish as long as one is willing to use multiple victims. The other side of the coin is that the stolen youth can also be leeched from the practitioner to add years as necessary. If I recall correctly, presenting as a child is an effective way to lure younger prey."

Pammy nodded solemnly.

Horrified didn't begin to express what I thought of that, but I managed to keep my face blank.

"Gregar has apparently stooped to unimaginable levels to associate with the darkest side of magic," Deval's mouth thinned as he spoke.

"Everyone walks the line, Deval. Don't be so shocked, but if he's assisted this family at all with their anti-aging regime, you had better bet that we will expect a resolution."

"Of course. That is if it's not moisturizer. Ladies." Deval stood and then looked over at me. "Peg, would you be so kind as to walk me to my car?"

"Uh, sure," I said, standing. I looked over at Pammy. "Don't let them clear my drink."

I walked with Deval but distinctively heard Pammy muttering behind me, "Off to have a tête-à-tête with the goblin prince, and she's worried about a half-finished coffee."

Damn straight I was. Deval held open the door, and I went out into the crisp, bright morning. I raised one hand, blocking the sunlight a bit to look for something black and luxurious. I'd started to step toward a sedan I'd seen him drive before he grabbed my hand and placed it through his own arm in an old fashioned gesture. I looked up at him.

"You are becoming quite adept at your job. I would, however, prefer to be notified when you literally have to kill yourself temporarily to beat back a curse."

"Yeah, I should have called, since it was in relation to the job for your mom, but since the meeting was this morning, I didn't see the need."

"I am your—friend. As a friend, I would like to be made aware."

"Well, friend, I appreciate your concern, and I will consider it, but I don't call up every friend I have when I've been in a dangerous situation. That's just my job, and that feels really time consuming for someone who can't decide what he wants." I removed my hand from his arm, turned, and walked back into the coffee shop. Pammy held up my latte and mimed drinking it. The scowl on my face broke into a smile as I rushed forward for my sugar and caffeine.

13

Pammy and Dorothy didn't say anything while I gulped down the now cold latte. I set the mug on the table and turned to look at the two women. "Don't say anything."

"Damn, Sug, you gotta go ruin my little ray of sunshine in this shit storm," Pammy grumbled but didn't ask about my conversation with Deval.

"I'm more of a spectator than a commenter," Dorothy added.

"I appreciate your restraint. So, Pammy, I'm going to pop over to the rental house for a little B&E. Care to join me?"

"That's my girl, right back into the fire. Don't mind if I do." She stood up, leaving her half-finished cup. Sacrilege in my book, but I refrained from commenting. "Dorothy, would you mind staying here this afternoon? I would like a presence available if someone wanders in. Your usual fee."

Dorothy grinned at us. "But, of course."

The two-story house I'd watched looked much the same except for the lack of vehicles. If they'd been home, I was feeling ballsy enough to walk up to the front door and ask to speak with Lola. It was what had I secretly hoped for, but this might be better. Pammy drove around the block twice before we parked a couple of streets down. The house looked empty, but we couldn't be certain.

The street itself didn't have any pedestrians on it. In the middle of the afternoon on a Wednesday, that wasn't unheard of, and it lent to our plans. We stood on the sidewalk outside the house.

"You wanna knock?" I asked.

"Scan the aura, Sug. See if there's anyone inside."

I pulled my magic front and center. It surged forward, no wards stopping it. My own wouldn't have allowed for this intrusion, but whereas there had been wards, all that were left now were remaining shreds. No life forces in the house.

"It's odd," I said to Pammy pulling my magic back to me.

"What's odd?"

"There are shreds of wards, but they're inactive. Even if they had deserted this house, I would expect them to leave them intact. Why go through the trouble to begin with if they aren't going to leave them up?"

I felt a tickle of magic as Pammy sent out her own less thorough feeler. "Huh, that does seem wasteful. Peg, why would a person with a devious mind leave a house wide open like that."

"A trap?" I responded hesitantly.

"Yep, they knew someone would come back to this house once the shit hit the fan. I sat in there with their matriarch and had tea. Lola surely told them, or at least her boy toy, that you had been watching the house. They've gone, but they're hoping to hit us with a surprise."

"Should we even go in then?"

"Hell yeah, we're going in. They are not more powerful than we are. They're just dirty players. Be careful, though. I have a few vials left, but Reaper doesn't grow on trees, and frankly I've never heard of anyone taking it more than once in such rapid succession. No need to pull on Death's whiskers."

We walked up to the front door, and I tried the knob, locked. Couldn't make it too easy. We looked around the street again, still empty of prying eyes. I followed Pammy around to the side gate. Like its neighbors, the house had a six-foot block wall with a sturdy wooden door, also locked. Pammy interlocked her hands and bent over. I looked at her.

"I'm too old to be boosted over fences but not too old to boost. Get over the damn fence."

No need to tell me twice. I put my booted foot in her hands and on the count of three felt myself projected into the air with more force than I expected. My palms scraped across the concrete blocks, and I winced but managed to scramble over the fence and shimmy down the other side. The lock consisted of a deadbolt rather than a padlock, convenient. I threw the bolt and Pammy stepped swiftly inside locking the gate behind her.

We walked along the cement pathway on the side yard to the back, which contained more cement, some gravel, and a fenced-in pool that looked green from misuse. If it had been someplace with colder climate, the seventy-degree weather during the afternoon would have been enough to use the pool, but Arizonans needed a cool ninety degrees to dip their toes in the "frigid" water.

The back porch held some cheap patio chairs. The

area wasn't dusty, so there had been some recent upkeep. We passed by the furniture to the sliding glass door. Pammy reached for the handle and it slid open without protest. She entered through the long vertical blinds.

"What are you waiting for?" she called back at me.

"I don't know, the all clear?" I mumbled as I pushed aside the blinds and entered.

"It's all clear," she snarked at me.

"Thank you, oh mighty leader," I snarked right back.

The lights were off, but the Arizona sunshine peeked through blinds on the many windows, so we were able to see the open kitchen and family room of the tastefully if sparsely decorated home, a common look for regular rental properties.

"You take upstairs while I search down?"

"You just don't want to climb the stairs," I said.

"I am perfectly capable of climbing stairs, young lady. I am in peak physical condition, but since you're here, you might as well get your youthful ass up the stairs."

I saluted her with, "Aye, aye, captain," and made my way to the staircase that I saw off the hallway from the kitchen.

"Be careful, Miss Sassafras," she called out behind me.

Her warning stopped me from taking the stairs two at a time as I'd intended. Instead I watched every step, pulling on my magic to try to see if there were any surprises set. I wouldn't be able to see everything, but some magics lingered. Either way, I needed to focus on my magic and my gut. The landing led to a hallway on both the right and the left to what I suspected were bedrooms. The center room was a bathroom, which I deduced with my mad investigator skills when I saw a toilet through the open door.

I entered the bathroom and flipped on the light, since I

couldn't see anything in the windowless room otherwise. I looked around at the standard lightwood cabinets, beige towels, and fiberglass tub and shower unit. The most interesting thing about the room was a cutesy sign above the toilet that referenced someone's aim to keep the bathroom clean and how your aim would help.

I looked in the shower, but other than a half-used cake of soap, there was nothing. The trashcan stood empty as well. I opened the drawers in the vanity to find a few random bobby pins. The mirror opened to reveal an empty bottle for aspirin. The previous inhabitants had cleared out, but I still hoped to find something that would clue us in as to where they'd gone off to. I entered the bedroom to the right of the staircase and headed for the closet. I'd been about to put my foot down when a mouse scurried out from the slightly open closet door. I let out a small shriek and stepped back just as the mouse ran into the jaws of a magical trap.

It let out its own shriek as the trap snapped shut. Briefly, I could see the writings flare up on the floor to reveal a set of runes before the magic pulsed briefly a dark purple and faded away leaving a singed carpet and a dead mouse.

"I'm sorry, Fievel," I said, quietly naming the mouse who had unknowingly sacrificed himself for me. "Pammy!" I called out.

"What?"

"I'm going to need you to climb those stairs."

I heard a grunt followed by the stairs creaking.

"In here, and be careful. You were right. The place is trapped."

Pammy came in and stood next to me to look at the mouse. "Was this already like this?"

"Nope, I'd been about to step into the closet when Fievel saved me."

She gave me an odd look. "You named the mouse?"

I shrugged.

"This is worse than I thought. I expected something, but death traps? What if a property manger or the owners came through? Can you imagine the uproar at a magical death of some landlord? We need to sweep the entire house."

"Weren't we going to do that anyway?"

Pammy rolled her eyes. "Yes, but not to the level that is now necessary. We'll need to do a life-force push."

"They went over that at the Boot Camp."

"Ever thought you'd need to do one?"

"Uh, not really," I said about the spell that involved taking a living being's life energy and pushing it outward. Usually an insect or a plant was used. "You have a potted daisy or scorpion you brought to sacrifice?" I asked.

"No, but I shoulda." She glanced around the room.

"There was a potted plant on the back porch. It might be dead."

"But if it's even half alive, we could use it."

"My thoughts exactly."

We trudged back down the stairs and then were careful to follow the path we'd both taken earlier out through the sliding door. Sure enough, there was a brown plant sitting in a big pot that would take two strong people to even shift. Upon further inspection, there was still some green to the plant that's outer leaves had seen better days. A twinge of guilt twisted my stomach about giving the plant that was clinging to life its final push to the other side, but we needed to clear the house.

"We don't need to bring it inside do we?" I asked, my only experience with the spell theoretical.

"Nope, which is good, since this sucker is going to take a lot of power, power that I'd rather not waste on moving it."

"What do I need to do?"

"You'll need to hold my hands and lend me your power."

I arched an eyebrow at her. Lending one's power took a lot of trust. I would be lending my magical life force; if I left myself open, nothing stopped Pammy from taking it all.

"Peg, if I wanted you dead, you'd be dead already."

Fair point. I held out my hands, and she grabbed mine. We stood on either side of the ceramic pot, our arms encircling the soon-to-be-dead plant.

Pammy looked me dead in the eyes. "Do not name the plant, Peg."

Sure, I hadn't been deciding between Dandy and Twiggy at that moment. Nope, no plant names from me.

I closed my eyes and did a mental check of my power and of all of the personal wards I'd built over the years through natural self-preservation and deliberate practice. It took time to open them to another person. I realized as I unlocked the final barrier how much I really trusted Pammy.

She felt the magical click as soon as I was open to her and began a soft chant in what I believed to be Latin. Spells didn't require a certain language, but if you learned it in another language, it wasn't necessary to translate to your own mother tongue, and if you weren't a scholar, that was also rather tedious. She continued on in the melodic chant. She spoke in a whisper, but her words boomed through my body as her and my magic blended together.

The spell called to the plant, requesting a sacrifice. The plant responded, and Pammy gathered its life force. It floated between us, a juxtaposition of small and infinite. With a final powerful chant, Pammy used our force to propel the plant's spirit into the house, pulling our own magic back, so we wouldn't suffer any adverse effects.

We stood there, both still open, waiting for a response. The magic pulsed three times. Once for each trap found. Momentarily stunned, I heard a ringing in my ears. Pammy gave me a quick shake, and I immediately pulled my magic back to me, shutting and locking every barrier I had back into place. I let go of her hands and sat heavily onto the cement porch, light headed. Pammy produced a candy bar out of nowhere and handed it to me.

I bit into the chocolate and peanut and caramel goodness. Though my body was still shaky, my mind began to clear. I looked up and saw that Pammy was leaning heavily on the pot and was eating another candy bar.

"You always keep candy bars on you? Wish I'd known. I'd come around more often."

"Ha. You mostly see me at Bump and Grind. If a coffee shop won't lure you in, a candy bar certainly won't."

I shrugged. "We need to get out of here soon. I couldn't take on a five-year-old human let alone a family of drainers."

"They've abandoned this house. It's doubtful that they'll be back, but you're right. It's better to be safe."

We went inside the house once more to locate the three remaining traps. One was in the master bedroom downstairs near the closet just as the one had been upstairs. The second was in the second upstairs bedroom in front of a desk. The third was trickier to find, but we eventually saw the telltale scorch marks in front of the garage door. *Glad we hadn't come in that way.*

We did a final quick search, but there were no other clues left behind. They'd cleared house. I took out my phone and snapped picture of the different traps through the house and produced a baggie for the dead rodent now known as Fievel. I wanted to know the exact cause of death. If we could identify the specific death traps used, we might be able to detect them more easily in the future.

As we left, through the front door this time, Pammy couldn't help herself. "This has been a dead end, especially for the plant and your mouse."

I didn't have the energy to laugh, but I gave her a small smile. "Can we stop by BBTT before we head back?" I asked, referring to the local witch crime lab and morgue, known as Boil Boil Toil and Trouble. The owners had a sense of humor.

"To get your mouse autopsied?"

"Yep."

"Good thinking," She peeled away from the curb.

Pammy parked right outside the front doors but waited in the car while I entered the squat brick building located on the outskirts of Phoenix. There were no signs advertising the building's name although the two vans out front had BBTT on their side panels because that was innocuous enough to not trouble the humans. I walked up to the front door and rang the bell. It took a few moments, but a man in a rubber apron appeared at the door.

Last time I'd seen Craig, he'd been picking up the body of a witch, so I was rather pleased that all I had to deliver today was a mouse.

Craig unbolted the double glass doors and stuck his head out. "Whatcha want?"

Pammy suddenly honked her horn, making me jump.

"Craig, why are you not letting my fortune in?" She called like a fishwife from her rolled-down window.

"Dammit, woman! I didn't recognize her. Why are you making a scene?" He called back just as loudly as Pammy before turning back to me. "Sorry, Meg is it?"

"Peg," I corrected.

"Right, like the pirate," he mumbled, opening the door to let me in.

"Sure like the pirate," I mumbled right back.

He went behind the front admittance desk. I stood in front of it and dropped the Ziploc baggie that currently held Fievel.

He looked at it. "It's dead, no charge."

"Yeah, I heard his death squeak. What I'm not sure of and don't have the time to check thoroughly is what curse was used. There were four set up in a rental home, and as you can guess, the sheriff isn't too keen on just letting some human moron get fried like this little guy. We want a full workup as to cause of death. If you can identify the specific curse used, even better."

"For a mouse?" He questioned me again.

"Do you think Pammy would chauffeur me with a dead mouse to the outskirts of Phoenix right before rush hour if she didn't want this done?" Really it had been my idea, but since she had in fact chauffeured me, I wasn't bending the truth too much.

"Okay, I'm billing this to the Arizona witches then?"

"Yup."

"Time frame?"

"The sooner the better."

"Fast means more expensive."

I was about to say we didn't care about expense, but then I remembered I wasn't in charge of the purse strings, so I marched back to the front door, opened it and yelled out. "How fast do we want it?"

Pammy turned down the oldies radio she had been listening to, asking "What?"

"How fast?"

"As fast as they can get it done," she hollered back.

"Fast means more expensive," I mimicked Craig.

"You tell Craig I know how much shit costs, and if he tries to gouge me, I will be calling his mama or invoking the Benevolence Act."

"What's that?" Any hesitance about yelling back and forth in a parking lot gone.

"We'll talk about it later. Go get your mouse sorted."

I turned and walked back to the counter. "Pammy said—"

"I heard what Pammy said," he cut me off. "I know it's serious if she brings my mother into it. Pam is usually a very reasonable woman." He took Fievel and had me sign a release form and provide my phone number for the results.

"If you can't reach me, please call Pammy. It's important."

"I know, like I said, she doesn't usually threaten to call my mother."

14

After a busy morning and afternoon, I had Pammy drop me back off at my car. She headed back into her unofficial office at Bump and Grind. I hadn't realized how exhausted I really was until she offered to buy me a coffee and I declined. Instead I went home, and after giving the fat orange tabby that greeted me at the door with a scratch, I grabbed a blanket, a mechanical alarm clock, and opened the lid to George.

Anyone not bonded with the safe would see a flat metal bottom. I saw carved stone steps. I laughed to myself as I descended into the depths of my plane. A month ago, descending the steps had filled me with trepidation. Made for a full-blooded goblin, the plane had been bitterly cold, and I'd nearly frozen to death the first time George had lured me in. Over time, the plane had gotten warmer. I still preferred going down in heavier clothing, but my sweater and boots along with the blanket would do.

The plane was a vast space filled with gray stone cut through with veins of blues, purples, and pinks. The sky a never-ending violet seemed to be forever caught on the edge of dusk. I found my favorite rock. Yes, I had a favorite rock. Long and flat, it was where I always rested or meditated when I came down here. I figured I would eventually explore further out, but for now, we were still getting to know each other and working on building trust. After all, I now planned on napping in the depths of the plane.

Time slowed on the plane, and it didn't do well with electronics. In the back of a closet, I'd found an old mechanical alarm clock that my aunt had left behind from when she owned the house, and it worked perfectly. I lay down on the stone, wrapping myself in the blanket like a burrito, after I'd set the alarm.

An hour later, the shrill clatter from the alarm clock woke me. I rose completely and ungroggily, as if I'd had a triple shot espresso and hadn't hit the jittery portion or the crash of the caffeine ride. Ready for round two, I stood up and blew a kiss to the air, thanking George for the pick-me-up, and climbed the steps with the energy of a Zumba instructor.

Cheddar met me with an affronted yowl when I exited the chest. Cheddar hadn't appreciated that I'd A) not invited him to nap time and B) failed to feed him after the affront of not being invited to nap. He could always tell when I napped without him. I glanced down at him guiltily, but I wasn't even sure if it was possible or safe for him to enter the plane. I'd ask Deval when I saw him next.

Thinking of Deval immediately sent butterflies to my stomach. I pushed away the feeling because it wasn't the time. Instead, I fed Cheddar a can of tuna, a treat that he'd become much too accustomed to. I'd begun to suspect his affronted yowls were really just his way of tricking me into giving him stinky fish. It worked. Cat placated, I headed out the door.

Dusk had come to the mortal realm along with traffic

as I headed to a townhouse development in the heart of Chandler. I managed to keep my spirits up despite the awful traffic and found myself in front of a security keypad a whole forty-five minutes later. I punched in the code and hit the pound sign. A breath of relief escaped me when the shrill beep indicated the gate was opening. I hadn't really thought that Lola would have the code changed on me, but apparently I'd been worried because I held my breath.

I pulled into the grouping of three-story condos that seemed somewhat exotic in a place that mostly held one- or two-story homes. After pulling into covered visitor parking, I approached the sea foam-green condo that belonged to Lola. Although she denied it, I still teased her that she'd chosen the color to match her eyes. I rang the doorbell and waited. Then I waited some more. After a few minutes, I rang it again.

Normally, I wouldn't just barge into my best friend's home despite having her key, but these were difficult days, and after having visited the McAllisters' rental, I no longer held any hope that they might have an actual soft spot for Lola. No one who was willing to set death traps for any unsuspecting person, or mouse as the case may be, had enough empathy to have a soft spot for anyone. So, I took out my keys and searched through the jumble for the pink sparkly number that she had gifted me. We'd both laughed at its gaudiness, but it was damn easy to find.

I unlocked the door and felt for her wards. I'd helped her lay them, and like with the gate, I was happy to find that she hadn't rekeyed them. A silly thought after only three days, but I'd never seen her act so erratic. I stepped inside and called out for her, but there was no answer. I walked through her home, very aware of the traps I'd come across earlier in the day, but if there were any, I didn't manage to set them off as I trekked up and down the three stories.

Lola enjoyed her shabby chic, and if it was white, pastel, distressed, overstuffed, tufted, or had an image of a flower on it, she probably owned it. After searching her whole house, I plopped myself on an overstuffed sofa only to have a fleeting idea. I walked up to a hall closet where I knew Lola stored her luggage set because I was too cheap to buy my own and had borrowed some from her on several occasions.

Opening the door, I pulled out a huge wheeled bag large enough to hold me. When Lola had first bought the lovely blue set covered in English roses, we'd drunk a bottle of wine, tucked ourselves into it one by one, and rolled each other around oohing and awing over how easy the spinning wheels made it to move a body. No, we weren't closeted serial killers. *If you couldn't be weird with your best friend then who could you be weird with?*

I placed the large bag on its back and unzipped it, knowing that the smaller bags in the five-piece set nested inside like a Russian doll. Opening the first suitcase, I found my answer. The second largest piece that could fit someone either very petite or under the age of fourteen by our estimation, was missing. Further unzipping found the smallest bag, a makeup case, also gone.

The missing luggage both relieved and terrified me. Relieved, because this meant that Lola surely hadn't gone unwillingly, since a kidnaper wouldn't be prone to letting a victim pack mascara and a curling wand. Worried, because now I really and truly had no idea where my best friend was. I looked at my watch. Seven p.m. on the dot. *It's seven p.m. Do you know where your best friend is?* No, I didn't.

I zipped the bag back up and returned to the sofa to "my" spot whenever we had a movie night. Lola would curl up on the other end of the sofa, and if we'd been kind enough to invite Bruce to watch whatever horrendously girly movie we'd chosen, he'd take the overstuffed wing-back chair with the tufted ottoman. Unsure of what to do, I continued to sit there as the dusk turned to dark, waiting for the doorknob to turn.

It had been meditative at first, but the longer I sat there, the more I began to stew in my own fear. The only answer to fear was to do something to combat it. I pulled out my phone and texted Deval. He hadn't said he'd be checking into Gregar's friendship with the blond male witch, but if I knew him, which I thought I did, then I suspected that he'd be tracking Gregar down to grill him. I texted him to ask if he had any updates.

I hadn't thought that he would actually answer, given the cold shoulder I'd been on the receiving end of recently, but thirty seconds later I had a text and a location. He hadn't had the chance, but Gregar was known to frequent a certain cigar bar in Scottsdale if I wanted to give it a go. I sat and stared at the message, feeling warm and fuzzy for a moment. Had Deval really just responded to me instantly and told me to go chase the bad guy on my own? His belief in me cut the fear like a knife.

I stood to leave but remembered that Lola could come home at any time with one of the witch family. I didn't want her to be alone if she did, despite her protests, so I called Bruce and offered him the use of an armchair for the night. You'd think I'd offered him a night's stay at a resort in Scottsdale with his chipper response. He just needed to feed his dogs and then he'd make the trek.

Instead of sitting in the darkness with my own morbid thoughts while I waited for him, I decided to make use of the extravagantly large television that Lola had hidden in an armoire. After all, I needed to find Bruce a chick flick so he wouldn't feel out of place. By the time he pulled his F-250 pickup into the parking lot, which I heard because the engine's rumble rivaled that of my own Jeep, though of course my Jeep was vintage, so I had an excuse, I had found a rerun of the *First Wives' Club* that had just begun.

Bruce rang the bell, and I let him in. He gave me a ridiculously good hug. He smelled like horses, hay, and dirt. He entered the living room and saw what I'd put on for him.

"I'd be annoyed at your presumptions, but damn if I don't love me some Bette."

"You and me both, buddy."

He took off his boots and settled into the chair, feet up. "You got some work to do, don't you? Shoo." He waved his hands at me.

I hesitated briefly. "You sure you don't mind waiting? I don't actually think she'll be back tonight. I'm just worried."

"I wouldn't want to leave her alone either now that we're officially staging an intervention. Even if she ain't back tonight, I'm going to eat her food and watch her TV. Mine's on the fritz, and I need to go to the library to restock my pile." The pile he referred to were the ten or so library books always strewn about his house.

"All right, you sure?"

"I said 'shoo,' and I mean 'shoo.' Get out." He leaned forward and pelted me with one of the throw pillows that previously adorned his chair.

I knew when I wasn't wanted.

15

I valeted and walked up to the cigar bar Deval had sent me the address to. Martin's was a one-story building with mid-century architecture and old school neon lights, which reminded me of something that fifties-era gangsters or the Rat Pack might frequent. I hadn't changed clothes, and the bouncer scrutinized my attire but let me in with a grunt that suggested I'd barely passed muster. These male-dominated clubs usually sought out women patrons for men to hit on when they realized that all the ogling wasn't going to get them a number from their server or bartender. It was not like I was wearing a T-shirt and flip-flops, but compared to the women walking around in short dresses and even higher heels, my fitted sweater, jeans, and boots made me appear a bit matronly.

Inside the cigar bar, it was, shockingly enough, smoky. All the expensive air ducts and ventilators in the world couldn't compete with a hundred people furiously lighting up at once. I let out a small cough and scanned the room. Blue lights above the stage that a jazz quartet played on backlit the smoke, giving the illusion of blue wisps flitting to and fro. The band was good, but I didn't feel like mingling.

From his reputation and our brief introduction, I'd assumed that Gregar would be front and center, so after scanning the room for a few minutes I finally looked to the darker corners and found him stashed in a velvet booth. *Huh.* I cringed to think at what it cost to clean their upholstery on a regular basis. I approached the booth. Unlike my meet with Vegard, I didn't feel the need to attempt an act because I wasn't here to ask him about the theft of the safe. I'd stay on witch topics, and he'd be none the wiser that we'd found the connection.

He sprawled along the back of the three-sided booth. In front of him sat a half-empty bottle of scotch. I assumed it was expensive, but for all I knew about scotch, it could be total garbage. His eyes were hazy, likely from the half-empty bottle, as he watched the band. He didn't notice me approach until I sat in the booth right next to him. He turned to stare at me.

"Hiya," I greeted as peppy as a cheerleader at homecoming.

His brows furrowed, "I've met you before."

"You sure have." I extended my hand. "Peg Darrow, Soldier of Fortune, Survivor of Reaper, Beloved of Vampires." That last part was on a whim but did make me sound more dangerous.

"So, you're a blood whore."

Well, that backfired. "I said Beloved. The feeling isn't mutual. So what are you up to, Gregar?"

"Trying to enjoy my solitude."

"Solitude is better suited for less popular locations. If you're going to attempt to go full hermit, why not find a lovely English garden with a cave?"

"Sometimes you can be alone while surrounded by people."

"How emo of you."

"Emo?"

"Never mind." I wasn't in the mood to discuss the varying subcultures if he hadn't bothered to stay hip with the kids.

"Well, fortune, I am not sure as to why you have approached me. You're an attractive enough woman, but I am not interested in witches."

"Try to contain your ego." I'd almost said 'how about witchlins' but held back. Pammy and Delmy seemed to want to keep that little bit of info under hat for now. Still, the intended offense was taken.

"Preference is not ego."

"No, your preference is bigoted. Your assumption that I had any interest in you whatsoever was ego, so let me enlighten you. I'm not interested in you either. Attractive enough but I'm not interested in assholes," I threw his own words back in his face.

"Rumor has it you've been seeing my cousin, so we both know that's not true."

"Fine, I don't mind occasional asshole tendencies, but the all asshole all the time thing doesn't work for me." Peg Darrow, master wordsmith.

He took a sip of his scotch, clearly unbothered by assessment. "So, you are dating him."

"No, I'm not, and I didn't come here to talk to you about relationship gossip."

"I'm not sure why I haven't had security remove you yet."

I wasn't either. "I'm the kind of obnoxious that people find endearing," I supplied helpfully.

"Keep telling yourself that."

"At this point, it's all I've got, but I do need to speak with you regarding a witch you may have known twenty years ago."

"Twenty years is a long time."

"It is."

I prepared for him to finally kick me out, but instead he waved down a waitress. "Please get the lady a drink."

The young woman, who obviously had won the genetic lottery with her lithe body on display in a tight black dress that barely covered her lady bits, smiled down at me.

"Shirley Temple, please."

Her smile grew wider at my childish order, but she didn't comment and sashayed away from the table.

"Did you really just order a Shirley Temple? Money is not an object. Get a thirty-year-old scotch for all I care." Goblins liked displaying wealth. It was part of their power source, and they liked to feel powerful.

"Gregar, normally I'd take you up on that offer, not in the scotch family but certainly a nice tequila, but I'm working, and who doesn't love a Shirley Temple?"

He didn't respond and instead pulled a cigar case out of his pocket, chose a cigar, clipped the end, and lit up with one of those torch lighters. His smoke now mixing with the other patrons' added a woodsy, spicy scent to the mix. I sneezed.

"Gesundheit."

"Thank you. So, why I'm here."

"Yes, yes, a witch I may or may have not known twenty years ago. Male or female?"

"Male."

"What did he look like?"

"Blonde, handsome."

"Not much of a description."

"Did you know a lot of blond witches twenty years

ago? I was under the impression you didn't associate with us much."

The waitress reappeared and dropped off my drink, asking if we needed anything else. Gregar sent her on her way. I sipped on the concoction that was all sugar and waited for a reply.

"You're right; I don't associate with witches much, and frankly I'm not sure why I'm associating now. Nothing but trouble, the lot of you."

"We're just people," I countered.

"You're people who couldn't control your own. I suspect this has to do with your matriarchal society. Can't keep a secret."

"Your own monarch is a woman. Would you say this to Delmy?" I barely contained an eye roll.

"Delmy is my aunt. I would tell her the same."

"Familial relationship aside, we both know that means 'no'. If you're so sure a king is better than a queen, why not rise up and put your money on the line." Peg Darrow, treason instigator.

"Again, speaking like a woman. These things are not so simple as that. There is a certain finesse to politics that you will never understand."

"Like paying a witch to have a scry spell set to spy on your cousin? Is that how a 'man' finesses politics? Seems cowardly to me and a touch juvenile, but being a woman a couple of centuries your junior, what could I possibly know?"

Any pretense at civility ended there. His skin reddened, which with the slight gray undertone the goblins sported, looked more purple. "How dare you!" He sputtered.

"I noticed that you didn't deny it. Is that another chapter in your misogynist playbook? When confronted by a woman, act outraged to avoid admitting what you've done. Your little friends didn't just set the scry. They've murdered a witch from the Arizona covens and left booby traps all over a rental home. You talk about our secrets being revealed and criticize us, but your recklessness could just as easily cause the same. The witches were outed over human murders. If some kids had gone in to hang out in the abandoned house and had been killed in those traps, do you truly believe the witches would be willing to shoulder all the blame?"

"Like you said, witches set the traps. This has nothing to do with me or my people."

"Not your people no, but you: you invited them here. I'm sure you welcomed them with open arms, knowing what they could accomplish for you. It only took one witch using dark magic to reveal our kind to the entire world after centuries of secret. It's a modern age, it would be even easier for you to be outed now."

"Are you threatening me?"

"You've threatened yourself with your own stupidity. So, I'll ask again. Did you know a male witch from two decades ago? He goes by Michael McAllister."

He rose abruptly and would have knocked over the bottle of scotch if I hadn't stopped it from teetering over. Stubbing out his cigar, he shuffled awkwardly out of the booth. I waited until he was clear of the booth before standing to follow him. The waitress approached him.

"What? Just put it on my tab," he snarled when she tried to collect on his bill.

"An automatic gratuity will be added if I do that."

"I don't care." He brushed past her.

No doubt she'd been hoping for something a little more than the standard twenty percent. If I'd had to deal with him, I'd want more, too. I gave her an apologetic look and scurried behind him. He didn't even realize I'd followed him until we were about ten yards into the parking lot.

He turned, his arm swinging to hit me with a right hook. I ducked, missing his hammy fist. I stepped into him and kneed him in the groin before placing my right booted foot behind and pushing him.

He landed on his back in the middle of the parking lot. The takedown would not have been so easy if he hadn't handicapped himself by drinking so heavily. He rolled around for the moment, clearly trying to compose himself, as much as a grown man who'd resorted to physical violence and instead been kicked in the nards could.

"So, you know the McAllisters; we already know that. What we don't know is where they are right now. Your little game with them is over, but my game has just begun. Please be so kind as to tell me what you know. I'm just a witch, but I'd be happy to call Delmy, then you can tell her what you really think and finally fight for what you falsely believe should be yours instead of scurrying around in the dark like a rat, letting us weak witches do your dirty work."

The look of hatred on his face as he struggled to roll over and stand up let me know that I'd made an enemy for life. I was okay with that. He managed to stagger to his feet when a bouncer approached us.

"You guys can't be fighting in the parking lot."

"Of course not, he fell," I responded.

"Fell right after he took a swing at you, and you kicked him in the balls. I admire your moves lady, but I can't have that in our parking lot."

"Oh, that just some stage combat. You'd never believe we were a couple of theater geeks, would you?" I put on a bright smile that didn't fool anyone.

Gregar was bent over at the waist, hands on knees, taking deep breaths.

"Listen, lady, I'm not a moron. I'm not calling the cops so long as you and this guy get out of here. He may be a regular, but he knows the rules. You got to get."

"We're getting. Give us two minutes to compose ourselves."

The guard turned away reluctantly but walked back up to the entrance where another bouncer waited as backup. I turned back to Gregar.

"Tell me what you know."

He stood straight up, his eyes flashing with anger as he jammed a finger at me. "I don't know any witches. Even if I did, I would never help you. So you and the other trailer trash can go back to hiding in whatever dump you crawled out of." Spittle had flown out of his mouth as he stressed his words. He turned suddenly and marched to the road where he hailed a taxi and got in.

That solved one problem. I'd been concerned I'd have to call on the bouncer to help me confiscate his keys. He thought he'd given me nothing, but I didn't live in a trailer, and I didn't know many witches who did besides Millicent in her youth. Some others here and there because you couldn't beat the pricing, but he'd told me to crawl back into my trailer as if that were the most common thing. I knew where to look for the family.

16

—————

Leaving the cigar bar, I felt like we were finally on to something. I also felt suddenly underprepared. We knew that the roving witch family targeted the weak and were unafraid of using spells and curses that would send a normal witch into hives at the possibility of the blowback. I'd known some darker practitioners in my day, but frankly, their practice was theirs and mine was mine. Never in all of the more extreme witches I had met would they have sunk to these depths of depravity.

Armed with uncertainty, I wished that Alice was still in town instead of gallivanting around, leading Fane on a merry chase. On the other hand, I couldn't help but be grateful that she distracted him at the moment because the last thing I needed to be added to my plate was my vampire stalker. A light bulb moment hit as I remembered that while Alice may not be physically present, her library was.

I considered calling Alice, but all I had was her home number. So, I called her friend and confidant instead.

"What you got?" Pammy answered on the first ring.

"A possible location of where the family may be hiding."

"That's good." Her voice practically purred.

"Yes and no. Gregar let it slip that the family was trailer trash in his mind, so I'm thinking RV Park or manufactured home lots."

"Well, that is looking for a needle in a haystack."

Arizona's dry weather meant that there were more than a few of these locations as withstanding tumultuous weather wasn't necessary in most of our state unless one counted one hundred twenty degree weather as tumultuous.

"Yeah, but it's a place to start. Remember Millicent said they had been in her childhood home. We could start there."

"Good idea. You ready to lead the troops on this one?"

"Actually, I had another idea."

"What's this idea?"

"We don't know enough."

"I'm listening."

"We know it's a family, but the only two who we've actually met are Michael, and you've met his mother. We don't know how many of them there are. We don't know the extent of their power or how the draining actually works since none of us are practitioners. I would really like access to Alice's library. A family like that, practically an urban legend, would have things written about them."

"Fair point. Let me make a call."

I was already in Tempe and didn't want to start heading east if I'd be heading west in a moment, so I pulled into a gas station and topped off the Jeep and got a jumbo diet Pepsi. Never could deny myself a fountain drink. Still waiting, I called Bruce to see if he had any updates. He didn't, but he was still watching TV. *First*

Wives' Club had ended, and something that sounded suspiciously like *Fried Green Tomatoes* played in the background. He was keeping to a theme.

I'd just hung up with Bruce when my phone buzzed announcing Pammy's call.

"You're keyed to the library."

"Huh?"

"Turns out Alice likes you more than either of us would have thought. Of course, sacrificing yourself to try to save her probably helped quite a bit."

My skin warmed in the sudden surge of pleasure I took at Alice actually giving me access to her library. It was almost unbelievable, but the surge of giddiness quieted as Pammy explained how to enter. All I needed to do was place my hand on the front door and use the pass phrase. The phrase made me hold back a snort. We hung up after that. Pammy's plan was to make a list of all of the trailer parks in the general Phoenix vicinity. I got to go read books. Obviously, I'd gotten the better task.

Twenty minutes later, I walked up to the First Baptist Church in Phoenix, having parked a few blocks down the road. To the casual observer, the building appeared to be a majestic ruin, its bell tower missing a good portion of its Saltillo tiles and the Italian Gothic architecture looking well and truly abandoned. Stepping up to the front door, I felt the magical facade dropped around me. The ruin had actually been magically restored to perfection, so while local politicians debated on what to do with the historically protected site, they had no idea that an "investor" had purchased the site decades prior and had gone about the restoration under the cover of magic.

The facade that still stood kept those unwelcome or unknown to our magic away from the largest deposit of books regarding the arcane in the entire Southwest. Alice's personal collection was a bit of an open secret. I'd been unaware of the presence of the library until last month and now I didn't know how I'd missed it, but most witches living an ordinary life unhindered by the demands of politics and enforcement or uninterested in general scholarship wouldn't know about it. And now I had an all access pass, at least until Alice returned.

I placed my hand on the large wooden doors and uttered the pass phrase. "Little pig, little pig, let me in." I managed to contain the laugh that wanted to escape with it. Magic surged from the door, trapping my hand against it. It traveled up my arm coating my entire body, pinning me in place. It became difficult to breathe as the magic searched me. It didn't feel malevolent, just verifying who I was. One hell of a security measure.

After what felt like minutes, the magic released me, and I nearly dropped the fountain soda I'd been clutching in my other hand. I gulped in air. On shaky legs, I entered the building. With a whoosh, the hanging candelabras ignited, casting a warm glow over the room. As with my other visits, I was momentarily awestruck at the grandeur of the space. The entry way was three stories high, done up all white in deference to the Gothic Moderne style. The ceiling sported long, dark wood beams holding the magical chandeliers hanging at various increments.

Only magic powered the house, making it truly off grid in the human sense. A heavy wood staircase led to the second floor landing, an open space filled with shelves and shelves of magical books. A previous visit had taught me there was even a cozy reading nook with a fireplace among the stacks.

Climbing the steps to the second floor, the stark quiet of the room and its vastness brought on a crushing sense of being completely overwhelmed. The tension that began to stiffen my shoulders multiplied once I stepped onto the landing and looked at the huge expanse filled with book after book after scroll. I swallowed. I'd only ever done research here with Alice present, and like the master librarian she was, she'd been able to traipse amongst the stacks, plucking titles with ease. The scary thing being that she didn't appear to grab those books with any mind to order, which meant it all came from her head.

Alice was endearingly referred to as bat-shit crazy. For my part, I considered it to be a term of endearment for the genius, if addled, mind Alice held, others maybe not so much. Taking a deep breath, I began to walk among the stacks. I wasn't really searching as of yet. Mostly I was looking to see if there was any rhyme or reason to the madness laid out before me.

There were indeed labels on the shelves, but to me they were nonsensical. Each row of shelves had a letter engraved into the wood—A through Z, but the labels for the shelves were labeled by strange "topics." Some seemed logical enough if slightly odd, to label an entire shelf for that subject "Cats" or "Bread," but then there were the truly odd labelings of "Oh No She Didn't" and "Pay the Price." All of these subjects appeared in no specific order, definitely not alphabetically according to the shelf layout.

I wandered down the length of the shelves, sure that this had all been a wild goose chase; then a little ray of hope hit me. At the very back of the shelves, wedged into a dark corner, sat an old-fashioned card catalogue. *Thank the gods.* It even had little scraps of paper and miniature pencils to write down locations. I pulled out the drawer labeled "M" and let out a breath of relief that it was alphabetical by actual subject and not the labels that appeared on the shelves.

I didn't hit the jackpot and find a subject labeled for the McAllisters, so instead I looked under "F" for families. I found several books that were on the subject of famous witch families and noted the rows and sections they were in. A particularly interesting one was labeled the "Dark Ones." Normally I'd think it was in reference to vampires, but the description labeled it as giving a history of the dark witches of the Americas. I used a miniature pencil to jot down the reference number and put a star next to it. I continued on, looking up various subjects, mainly curses and dark magic. When I had ten books listed, I figured that was more than enough to get me started.

Finding the books took time because even though I had the rows and the subjects listed, as previously observed, the subjects weren't in any order that made sense to my brain. I did laugh a little when I pulled *The Dark Ones* from the "Oh No She Didn't" subject shelf and continued on grabbing the other books as I found them. By the end of my search, I'd located every book except for a small volume on curses. I gave up after twenty minutes because I had three volumes on the subject, it was already looking to be a long night, and all I'd brought by means of caffeine was a jumbo diet Pepsi that was now half gone.

My finds were all gathered next to a wingback chair in front of the fireplace that had lit along with the candles, giving off cozy heat. I sat and pulled out a three-subject notebook I'd taken to carrying whenever I had my purse. Flipping the book to the final section, I grabbed my pen and pulled the first book from my stack at random, one of the curse volumes, and began my labors.

Three hours later, I was tired, out of soda, and had to pee. I'd never used the bathroom here, and finding it might require a ball of string, a toll for a mystical creature, and my blood for all I knew, but I needed to make the quest because the night was not over. I was relatively sure I hadn't encountered a doorway to a bathroom while I searched the stacks, so instead, I went to the front of the landing to a corner with an entryway that led off to what I assumed was Alice's personal quarters.

"I'm not snooping. I just have to pee," I said out loud as I entered the hallway. Silly though it may be, it never hurt to make your intentions known in a place as magically charged as The First Baptist Church slash Secret Witch Library. A light suddenly appeared in an open doorway. My magic jumped in my palms at the unexpected light.

"Is anybody here?" I called out, "Like I said I'm just looking for a bathroom."

When no one responded, I warily continued down the hall toward the room. My back to the wall, I slid along cautiously as I looked in the room. Porcelain gleamed in the form of a toilet. I let out a sigh of relief. The house had just been directing me to my stated desire. I went in and closed the door. Paranoia had me looking behind the heavy shower curtain around the claw foot tub before I sat down to do my business because I didn't need a *Psycho* experience to add to the atmosphere of the day.

After relieving myself and washing my hands, I stepped out to the hallway, about to head back to my books, when a moment of genius hit me.

"Any chance a girl could get a cup of coffee?"

Another light turned on at the end of the hall. Giddy, I walked down to the new light source. The bathroom light turned off as I walked away, which spooked me a little but not enough to stop my coffee mission. I walked into a kitchen that was set up a bit like an office break room given the smattering of tables and chairs on one side, but unlike offices, these were all heavy, dark wood and not plastic, metal, and laminate.

I imagined Alice holding study sessions in here, but really I'd need to ask her how often she needed seating for thirty at the library. Turning from the tables, I spotted the object of my desire on the stone countertop. A coffee pot sat in the center. Walking over, I found that the cabinet above it labeled "coffee supplies," no ambiguity here. The coffee maker was a standard model, and I easily placed the filter, grounds, and water before hitting start. Among the supplies there was sugar along with sweetener. Even better, I found a variety of flavored creamers when I opened the fridge.

I selected a cinnamon chocolate number, and while the coffee brewing made its beautiful music of hisses and gurgles behind me, I felt I had hit the mother lode. Next to the fridge, sitting on a glass pedestal complete with cover, sat a loaf of cinnamon bread. I debated whether it was appropriate to pilfer bread along with coffee when I saw the framed sign above it. *Help Yourself. Magical Minds Need Magical Bites.*

If rumors were true, the bread was magical in the sense of being delicious beyond reason, so I lifted the lid and ripped off a chunk of the pull-apart bread, taking a healthy bite. Butter, cinnamon, sugar, and bread, hit my senses in a combination that stood up to the hype. I set the remaining chunk down on a paper towel, determined not to eat the entire stash like a heathen and deciding to ration what I'd already taken.

Back at the chair with my snacks, I went into overdrive. I found five curses that were likely candidates for the death bombs left at the rental, and as if reading my mind, my phone buzzed with a call from BBTT.

"Hello," I answered.

"Hey, Peg, got your results on the mouse. Nasty business."

"Yeah, his death squeak led me to believe it wasn't a pleasant death."

There was a pause on the other end. "Yeah, okay, so the mouse's heart literally exploded."

"Cor Contractus," we said at the same time.

"Why'd you have the mouse autopsied if you already knew?" He sounded exasperated.

"I didn't know his heart exploded, but I have been researching death curses, so when you mentioned an exploding heart, I figured."

"Well, there you go. Please do me a favor and make sure Pammy knows I called you. I don't need her calling my mom."

"Of course."

We exchanged goodbyes, and I hung up. I sent a quick text to Pammy, *Craig came through. It was the Heart Break Curse.* I translated the Latin.

I got her response quickly. *Good, I didn't really want to call his mother, but you can never back down on a threat. Not so good about the curse.*

Pammy liked to pepper in little Fortune lessons here and there. I repeated, "don't make threats that you don't follow through on" a couple of times. She also enjoyed pointing out when anyone failed to pick up on her subtle lessons. Really, I needed to add a section to my notebook and call it Pammy's Tips and Tricks to Succeed at Being a Soldier of Fortune. I almost opened to a new section to add that but shook my head and dug back into the books.

The curse books held no information regarding draining. So taboo was it in our society that I could learn how to literally make someone's heart explode, but that book considered draining too hardcore. Draining was the curse that had led to our outing and the end of our thousand-year life span. One of our leaders in Salem, Massachusetts, had fallen in love with a mortal man. Rather than enjoy the years she had with him, she decided that draining other humans to stop his aging was a good idea.

She might have gotten away with it if she'd gone after the old or the sick, but she wanted a more powerful life source and chose the children of her enemies. *Not a shining pillar of witchhood.* She got caught, hanged, and decapitated, but not before she outed all of the witches because they did not defend her indefensible acts.

The witches helped the villagers stop her, feeling safe behind the protection of being nearly immortal. She took that away from us because the most evil among us are often the most powerful. Before her curse, it would take a beheading or setting someone ablaze until nothing remained but ashes.

It was easy to see why the spell had been pretty much erased from our history, but the problem with censoring something was that it limited the people who had access to the information. It did not sit well with me that McAllisters were the only family that knew of the spell. Pammy had thought that the counter-spell was lost, but if anyone had it, Alice would, so I continued to comb through the books.

Well after midnight, my third cup of coffee from the pot had grown cold, and my eyes struggled to stay open, but I'd finally reached the last book in my pile, *The Dark Ones*; and eureka! Right in plain print were the histories of some less than savory witch "families" including the group I was looking for. The book implied that they were a cult with a turnover in membership given the longevity, but as I read, given what I knew I had a niggling feeling that the rotating cast of characters had simply taken on new names and not been replaced entirely.

A matriarch always led the family and though that was the norm in witch culture, the descriptions of the leaders through time mirrored each other, and they all noted reports of the woman losing decades of age seemingly overnight. This was often at a glance before the family moved on. One such encounter had been found in a journal had been excerpted in the book.

Mary McGowan came and stayed with us for a summer. She claimed to be kin of our grandmother who had passed the year before. Her elderly and fragile appearance along with the stories she shared with us about our grandmother led us to offer the woman shelter, but she had odd ways about her. She was friendly at first, but after we welcomed her into our fold, she became removed and distant.

The only person she remained friendly towards was our youngest, Hillary. Every day she'd play with that girl and tell her stories. Twice we found them out of bed going for late night walks to find fairy circles. We had to ask the woman to not do that anymore, since it always gave me a fright. Two months into her stay with us, I found her bag by the front door, and when I saw her come down the stairs, I was in for a shock.

Gone was the fragile old woman with steel-gray hair. Her thick braid now a lustrous brown, her gait unfettered by age, her face unlined. If it weren't for the piercing blue eyes, I would never have recognized her. I questioned her on it, and she admitted that her side of the family had a secret for a fountain of youth, and she'd simply needed time to gather her vigor.

I wanted to question her further, but suddenly there was a wagon that held eight of her kin, all strong, young witches. I asked her if she wanted to say goodbye to Hillary, but she just replied that she already had her goodbyes with the girl and left in a whirlwind, not even introducing her family.

It was not until hours later that we realized the absence of our child. I knew in the heart of a mother what had happened, and I spread the story far and wide. I can only pray that the woman and her family met a miserable end because it is clear now that the story of being family was just another strand in the web of deceit and evil that she had weaved.

Similar accounts spread throughout the book. The names changed, the mysterious youthful transformation was usually present as well. The matriarch was always present, but it seemed that her followers varied other than a man I assumed to be Michael and the total number of nine witches, three sets of three. Nine could be a powerful number allowing three circles at any given time.

The final chapter ended, as the others had, with witches missing. The entire book focused exclusively on tales of drainers, and as I flipped to the last page, I found a yellowed piece of paper folded and wedged in the crease next to the spine.

Scanning the document, my eyes widened. It was a reversal spell. Pammy had said it was impossible, but my magic tingled just reading over the incantation. I thought it could be the real deal. The lethargy I'd been feeling faded quickly as I transcribed the spell into my notebook. I replaced the original into its hiding place, closed the book, and closed my notebook, knowing it held something precious and rare. I cleaned up my coffee mug and pot and re-shelved my books, leaving the space the way I had entered it.

As I left the old church building, I clutched my purse to me. I knew this wasn't the only copy of the spell, but it felt fragile. If I didn't get it to the other Arizona witches before our final showdown, I didn't know that anyone ever would with Alice being gone right now. So I got in my Jeep, turned on the engine, and locked all my doors before texting the spell to Pammy. I then sat and memorized the counter curse. Given its oddly simplistic nature, it made sense to have it ready to go if the McAllisters found me before I found them.

An earlier lesson from Pammy, *paranoia was being prepared*. She likened it to television thrillers where some idiot would get secrets vital to national security and for reason X, Y, or Z never disclosed said secrets, gets killed in a fireball, and then everyone's screwed for six episodes for something that could have been resolved with one phone call. One of my daily goals was to not be *that guy*. I sent a second text stating that the family had gone by different names over the centuries, but they always had nine members. Then I signed off because the clock read two a.m., and a witch worth her mettle knew that she needed to keep her energy stores up.

17

My kitchen table was small, and every spot of it was covered in various notes, my laptop, and Cheddar, who was supporting my work by sitting on whatever piece of paper I was currently looking for. I'd called Pammy when I'd woken up after four hours of blissful sleep to verify that she'd gotten my text. She had, and she emailed me a list of the trailer parks that she and whatever people she'd roped into the search, had found. I continued my search to make sure the list was as thorough as possible.

An hour into my search, my doorbell rang. Being in the zone, I keyed into my wards to verify a magical presence, not in the mood to open the door for anyone selling religion or even Girl Scouts cookies. Yep, I was that in the zone. But it was a goblin, so I felt obligated to answer it. Surprise, surprise, it was Deval, and he'd come bearing gifts. I took the thirty-two-ounce iced coffee concoction without a word and turned to head back to my workspace, leaving the door open for him to follow.

I heard the door close and footsteps behind me, so he must have gotten my silent invitation. I lifted the mug and empty coffee pot I'd set on my kitchen table on the counter, since they had a replacement, and returned to my seat. Deval took the chair across from me on the small, round four-top table. Cheddar sat in front of Deval and started his motor when Deval began to scratch behind his ears.

"Thank you for the caffeine."

He eyed the empty pot that I'd place on the counter. "Maybe it wasn't a good idea. You'll crash if you keep this up."

I shook my head. "Nope, I've reached the point of no return. I must crawl into the crevasse, because there's no hope in turning back."

He completely missed the sitcom reference or chose to ignore it. "Have you heard from Lola?"

"Not a peep. I went to her house yesterday, and two pieces of her luggage set are missing, so I don't think that she left under duress, but this family lulls their victims into a false sense of security, so luggage choices can mean absolutely nothing. I've got Bruce sitting on her house now."

"I spoke with her parents this morning. They've been difficult to track down."

I'd considered reaching out to Lola's adoptive family but remembered that Lola had mentioned a long winter vacation in Europe, which was why she'd planned on Christmasing with my family in Tucson. We weren't religious per se, but we liked feasts, presents, and over-the-top decorations as much as the next guy. "I'm glad that you did. I should have, but it's been a whirlwind, and I don't know them well. I'm not even sure if I have their numbers."

"They were distraught at this news, her mother particularly. The deaths of Lola's biological parents never felt quite right to her, which may be why she didn't spend too much time integrating Lola with other witch families. I hadn't realized that you're her only close witch friend."

I shrugged. "One good friend is better than a dozen acquaintances."

"Agreed, and needless to say, they were concerned about this family, particularly when I mentioned the child-hood connection. They've requested that we find her and force her away from these people, even if it's against her will."

"Already the game plan, Buck-O, but we've got to find her first. I found a lead when I went to talk to your cousin yesterday."

"Buck-O?"

"I said I had a lead, and you focus on a nickname?"

"It was just odd; continue about your lead."

"Gregar was pretty adamant that he didn't associate with witches for the most part, but when I got him riled up, he did say that he wouldn't associate with trailer trash. You remember that I told you that Millicent had first run into the witches when living in a mobile home park?"

"Yes."

"The way we figure it, they've gone back to their roots. I think it could be either RV or manufactured home, but really with a family that has to move often, I'd say that a large RV would make more sense. Disconnect a few lines, and you are ready to move your house."

Lost in thought, he'd stopped petting Cheddar for a moment. The orange tabby batted at his hand to remind him to keep petting. Deval absentmindedly started scratching him again. "Yes, that would make sense. When are you going to begin this search? I'd like to accompany you."

I handed him the printouts I'd made so far. "I'm just finishing up my list. It's good that you came to volunteer. I was going to ask Bruce, but I'd rather that he stayed at Lola's, and Pammy and I have decided that it's not safe to go alone. She'll be taking Dorothy."

"That suits our purposes. When do we leave?"

"I need a few more minutes to make sure that I haven't missed any place and then divide up the list and email Pammy her half. Also, just as a check in, I'm not ignoring the job with your mother. If we find the McAllisters, we can get a verification of who paid to set the scrying spell in your house, then Blam-O, thief caught."

"You're using a lot of nonsensical words that end in O today."

"Like I said, Deval, I need to crawl into the crevasse. We're so close, but we need to get every detail right."

He nodded and stood, which got a growl instead of a bat this time. Deval ignored Cheddar. "I'm going to call my mother and Griselda and give them updates about where you are in the investigation."

"Much appreciated." I waved him away and worked to finish my search.

We were on park number twenty of thirty. We'd started out the search hopeful, and somewhere deep inside me, there was still a whisper of hope. I knew that results didn't usually happen on the first try, and that Murphy's Law would indicate that we wouldn't find our prey until the very last location, but I'd ordered the spots on our list based on the ones I thought had the most potential for hiding an evil coven of RVers.

Pulling into a run-down mobile home park at the very edge of East Mesa, I'd been surprised to find a large number of shiny new RVs present along with older, sagging manufactured homes. I'd thought that this location didn't have RV hookups for rent, but the sign out front advertised otherwise. The Internet had failed me in this instance.

"Do you see that?" I pointed the sign out to Deval. It appeared that we both got quiet when things felt dire, so the trip so far had been particularly quiet.

"I do." He looked over at me and smiled.

His smiles were rare, and it made me want to jump on him, but instead I held myself in check, unbuckled my seatbelt, and got out of his SUV that we'd driven on this excursion. I'd thought about arguing that he always got to drive but changed my mind and decided to not offer to pay for gas instead.

The dirt parking lot had a small trailer toward the park entrance labeled "Office." We'd popped into the office at the first few locations but found the property managers relatively unhelpful. We'd either had to pretend to be looking for a home or a parking space, which then entailed getting stuck on a tour that we didn't want to take, or worse, we indicated that we were looking for someone, at which the office managers had clammed up. The one and only location I'd made that mistake at ended with Deval having to park on the opposite side of the site and boost me over the cement wall that surrounded it, so I could search the area. I'd gotten really good at being boosted over walls in recent days and practically flew over. We were both grateful that I hadn't broken my neck.

This time around, as we had done with the past dozen, we'd simply pulled in and walked out like we were visiting someone. The name of this park was Desert Heat Mobile Home Park. The name was fitting because there were no trees planted to provide shade in the blistering summer months. We started down the first of the dirt-paved roads.

Deval was on high alert, and I pushed my magic out a little. I didn't want to announce our arrival if we found the family, but I needed to get a read on anything magical that we came across.

We'd walked down two of the streets of the park, and despair was again beating out hope just as I felt the tickle of magic. I held my hand out, hitting Deval in the chest to stop him, and reached out a little further with my senses before picking up where it came from. I pointed to the side-by-side doublewides down the road a bit.

"Do you feel them?" He asked.

"I feel magic, but I can't be sure it's them, plus we'd guessed at RV. The only way these could be taken out is if they hired a semi. The McAllisters didn't strike me as the types to have time to put that much effort into their movement."

Deval looked over at me. "Perhaps they own a semi?"

I thought about it for a moment. "If they've been alive as long as I suspect, I have no doubt that they have the money to own a fleet of semis. It just seems impractical for their lifestyle. They'd want a faster get up and go. I'm sure they've run into the cavalry before, their changing lineup attests to that, so they'd want to be able to get gone in ten minutes."

He nodded. "But you sense witches?"

"Yes."

"Let's talk to them. They may know something."

"Of course." I headed up to the first trailer and climbed the rickety steps leading to the front door. I wasn't against a manufactured home for an affordable domicile, but this one was in bad shape. The siding was peeling, and it somehow sagged in the middle. I wasn't even sure if the stairs leading up to it could hold me and Deval at the same time, so I motioned for him to stay on the ground for a few.

I knocked directly on the front door because the screened door had been slit down the front. I heard hushed chattering inside that reminded me of squirrels arguing over a peanut. After a few moments, the chattering stopped, and the door was opened just a crack. Through it I saw a witch. Her skin was pale and slack on her face, her eyes sunken, sporting dark circles, and what little I could see of her hair in the shadows of the home was stringy and greasy.

I'd seen this before, and seeing it now hit close to home. This was what my aunt had looked like when we'd finally managed to pull her out of the Arizona vampire nest. I knew vamps kept their blood donors in different locations, but I didn't think they'd keep them in total squalor. Guess I'd been wrong to expect any sort of decency from them.

"Hi, my name is Peg. I'm a fortune, and I just wanted to check up on your group here. See if there's anything you needed assistance with." It wasn't the reason that I'd knocked on the door, so that part was a lie, but I would help them if I could and given the state of the woman at the door and the earlier indecipherable chatter, I'd do better with this approach than outright interrogation. I must have said the right words because the door flew open.

"Who's that guy? He's not a fortune."

"He's not even a witch." Another head popped up from behind the first.

"That is Deval. He's a goblin," I said the latter in more hushed voices, not wanting my voice to carry given the tightly packed homes.

Behind the women, we heard the muttering start again. "A prince, a prince! He will find her. He won't be mad at us when he comes back if we find her. The prince will help. The fortune will help!"

I had meant it when I said that I would help them if I could, but I'd been hoping they would ask for money or a ride to the store. It sounded like we'd just found another kettle of fish, but I put a smile on my face, a woman of my word.

"May we come in?" I asked.

The woman who opened the door stepped back, to let us in. Deval waited until I stepped into the trailer with spongy floors before he alighted the steps. There was no foyer in the home, and I walked straight into a dim living room, the only light escaping from behind a single window's threadbare curtain and the a lamp in the corner that had a bulb that couldn't be more than twenty watts. I considered asking them to find another light source but then remembered my aunt when she'd first come home.

Vampires couldn't be turned like was believed in popular fiction. They were born, but just as in the way that vampires could temporarily steal witch magic, albeit in its weakest form, when they got a witch hooked on their blood, they also gave witches some side effects such as their dislike of light. Vampires were perfectly capable of going out in the sunlight, another falsehood, but they were nocturnal by nature, and like the parasites they were, they only seemed to pass on the worst of themselves. I stepped into the living room and went to an older sofa. I couldn't tell in the shadowed room, but I thought it was a plaid fabric.

"Mind if I sit?"

"Sit, sit," three of them said at once.

So I sat on a corner spot. Deval came and chose to stand next to me.

"Ladies." I spotted lone male witch standing in the

corner. "And gentleman. You said there was a witch missing?"

"Yvette!"

"Yvette! They took her. Pretended to be our friends."

"But they took her!"

Everyone chimed in, making it difficult to understand what had happened to Yvette.

"We will help, but we need to understand exactly what is happening. Who leads you here? Have one person speak." Deval's voice boomed through the room.

"I will speak." The woman who answered the door stepped forward. Despite her haggard appearance, she was still the least skeletal of the bunch, her eyes a little less sunken, her hair not as thin as the other donors in the room.

"What's your name?" Deval asked to the woman.

"Nora." She shuffled closer and sat in a wooden chair in front of the couch.

"Did a vampire take Yvette?" I asked.

Cries of "No" sounded from the peanut gallery, but Deval held his hand up and looked at Nora.

"No, if our vampire was here, he'd never let them take Yvette, but he is gone and won't answer when we call."

I had a bad feeling. "Who exactly is your vampire?"

"Fane." The others sighed in contentment at the mention of his name.

"Great, so if another vampire didn't take Yvette, do you know who did?" I prodded.

"Witches!" Nora cried, "They were worn like us. We thought they were like us, but we don't take in other witches. They pretended to be our friends."

Deval gave me a weird look. "It's really odd how every fucked up aspect of your life seems to be converging on itself to wrap itself into a tidy bow."

I gave him an incredulous look. "Not my fault."

He sighed. "I know that. It's just odd."

We turned back to Nora, who had wrapped her arms around herself and began rocking back and forth. Crap, I didn't need her to go into a catatonic trance right now. I snapped my fingers. "Nora! I need you to focus. Tell me about the drainers that were here."

Her head snapped up, and she stopped rocking. "You said drainers. Drainers are bad. Fane will be so upset that we let them get to her."

"Whereas I appreciate your concern for your future relationship with your dealer, I'm a little more worried about Yvette."

Nora flinched despite her dazed look, and my face heated with shame. I'd meant to say witches, not drainers. These people were in the throes of addiction and some diseases were harder to fight than others. They didn't need my reprimand or the added burden my slip had caused them.

"I'm sorry, Nora, I didn't mean that as harshly as it sounded."

"S'okay," she mumbled, her head down. I heard the tears in her voice.

"I really am sorry, Nora. My family has its own history with Fane. I know it's very hard to think of other things when you've been bitten on a regular basis, and that it's even harder to leave, but you're a witch, and as a fortune, I will do what I can to help you. How long has Yvette been gone?"

Her chin trembled, but she gave a weak shake of her head, reaching her hand up to wipe away her tears and looked at us. "She's been gone twelve hours."

"Is that unusual?" Deval asked.

"Yes, we are to stay in the house unless we need food.

Right now, we have permission to leave the house to buy food or necessities like toilet paper, but we must go straight to the store and come straight home in case Fane returns."

"Are you not always allowed to do these things?" Deval asked when he caught the "right now" part of the sentence.

She shook her head, wringing her hands. "No, if he is home, his people will bring our things, but before when he went away, we were forgotten. This time he did not forget, but he will be home soon, so we must hurry back if we go out."

I didn't think she meant soon as in hours because I knew Alice was still leading him on a wild goose chase, so I didn't worry about her words.

"Can you tell us about the witches you thought were your friends?"

"Yes, they came in last week."

"Are any of them still here? I noticed a magical signature on the trailer next door."

"That's ours too. They had an RV, a real nice one. I thought they were like us."

"What do you mean like you?"

"They were really thin and looked like maybe they also belonged to a vampire. When we asked, they said they did and that they traveled around with him. I thought that was odd because we never saw another vampire, but Fane always says that vampire business is not our business, so we didn't meddle, but the witches seemed really nice."

"Did you ever go over to their place?"

"Yes, they cooked and made extra for us a few nights. They were really nice, especially to Yvette."

"Is Yvette younger?"

"Yeah, she's the newest. She's Fane's favorite. The

newest is always the favorite because they aren't so worn out."

That was an interesting self-observation from a woman who didn't seem completely there.

"Why do you think they took her?"

"She went to the store with one of the guys from the family. We heard some noises and looked out the window. They were all packed up and pulled away. Yvette never came back."

"Are you sure Yvette just didn't go home. You can break the addiction. My aunt did."

Nora's face shot up to me my eyes. I saw mixture of disbelief and fear. "No, no, the master says we are his now and forever. Yvette knew this."

I let it go. "Why didn't you call Pammy when you couldn't get ahold of your master?"

She looked genuinely surprised at the question. "We are his now. The witches wouldn't help us."

"Then why am I here?"

"I don't know."

"Honestly we were looking for the witches that took your friend, but I'm a fortune, and I know Pammy really well. No matter what your master says, you are witches, and Pammy will help you. If you want to leave, Pammy can help you. She will help you."

There were some mutterings behind her both angry and hopeful.

"No, I must stay, but you can find Yvette, and it will be better then."

"Okay, if that's what you want, but if you change your mind, Pammy will come and get you, no questions asked."

"And how will she protect us once she gets us?" Nora snapped.

"She has in the past, and she will now." I left my

answer deliberately vague, knowing that Pammy wouldn't want people so close to the vampires to know about the various safe houses and rehabilitation centers across the country. If these witches called Pammy, they'd find out about them once they were safely out of harm's way. "What did the RV look like?"

"Shiny."

"Like an airstream? Silver?"

"No, I'd never seen one painted all black. It was black and shiny and big."

"It had heavy curtains." Another voice came from behind Nora.

"And custom black rims."

"It's unusual to have an all black RV?" I asked, completely unfamiliar with the norms of the recreational vehicular world.

"This one was all black. No details. Normally it has a swoosh or something." Nora took control of the conversation again.

"Right. Okay," *black, got it.* "I'll let you guys know when we have news."

"Good or bad?"

"Good or bad," I agreed.

18

***

W hen I got into the SUV, I melted into the seat, not realizing how emotionally draining the encounter would be with so many troubled witches after a long morning of searching. Deval climbed into the driver's seat and gave me a concerned look.

"How are you holding up?"

"Fine, but I need to take a nap in George." I shouldn't have said that.

"Why is that?"

"It's just my safe place," I said as a half-truth. I didn't know if it mattered that I got supernaturally charged from the plane despite it not holding untold amounts of riches, but I liked to keep some things close to my chest.

"I'm glad you find comfort in the space. Goblin children often retreat to theirs for comfort."

I looked over from my slumped position giving him the stink eye. "Are you calling me a child?"

He sighed. "I was not calling you a child. I was telling you a cultural norm of my people, or your people, in which I thought you might be interested."

I looked out the window. "Sorry, it's been difficult to speak with you lately."

"When has our relationship not been difficult?"

"Good point. We should probably stop making out against cave walls."

He remained silent for a moment. "It's not a cave."

"Deval, it's a cave. A super fancy, schmancy cave. The fanciest cave I've ever seen, but still a cave, and that is what you chose to talk about in that sentence?"

"Well, I'm not going to agree that we shouldn't make out against walls. It's something we should both think on when we're not in the middle of possibly catastrophic events. I'm not avoiding you because I'm uninterested. I've avoided you because I want to come at this with a level head and think you should, too. We could ruin our friendship."

I snorted. "I think you ruined our friendship when you kissed me last month, and I'm fine with being just friends, Deval, but you need to stop sending mixed signals. I'm not one of many. I'm all or nothing for however long we're together. So, don't kiss me, ignore me, show up with another woman to an event you know I'm likely to attend, then come at me in a sexual frenzy only to leave me hot and bothered, and then avoid me for two days. By the way, I've been told what it means, that magical make-out session brought on by your own plane."

He stared straight ahead not making eye contact. "Yes, it means something, but it is not all binding. It is something we need to discuss, to decide upon because once we realize how good it could be without any thought to the fallbacks, we're stuck because we won't want to give up on it no matter how bad it gets."

"So, you think it would be bad?" I questioned him.

"I just don't know, Peg."

"Fine, we can talk about it after this is all over, Lola is safe, and your mother writes me a huge check."

We didn't speak during the rest of the trip because even though I'd never been good at the silent game, lately with him, I had no problems. I wasn't sure if that was good or bad.

After being dropped off at home, I called Pammy.

"Talk to me."

"I just got home."

"You found something, or you went through your list?"

"I found something." I gave her the description of the witches that we'd found and what they'd told us about their missing friend.

"God damn it, I didn't realize he'd started a nest. Clever of him to put it in the middle of a trailer park."

"Why's that?"

"Vampires like luxury. They don't live in squalor. Now, they control high-end clubs and drug rings. They used to use Opium Dens to make their money and bring in willing feeders. It's why they use the poppy as their symbol."

"I did know that."

"I know you do. I'm just talking out loud because I'm mad. Fane knows I won't stand for it, and half of those witches will die from the withdrawal."

"You won't leave them with him?" I asked not really sure how this worked for the willing participants.

"No, they're dead with him no matter what. If I take them, they at least have a chance. Plus you remember the lesson."

"No signs of weakness to the enemies."

"Good girl. I'm going to call out an APB on the RV.

We'll have to get the enthralled when this is all over. Luckily, Alice mentioned that she planned on really screwing around with Fane for a bit, so we have at least a few more days."

"Good to know," I murmured.

"Yes, that does mean once we wrap this bitch up, you may actually have a few days free of jobs, training, and a vampire stalker. For now, rest up; I need you at your full power when we find the McCallisters."

"Okay, but what did you mean by an APB? We don't work with law enforcement."

"You'll find out soon enough, and I'll be needing a nap as well when it's all said and done."

We hung up, and I went about my routine prior to going to visit George, using the bathroom, finding my thick blanket and alarm clock. I didn't get cell phone reception in the goblin plane, so I would limit myself to an hour, enough to charge my batteries to full with hopefully a minimal chance of missing the action. It couldn't be helped either way. I needed to get my strength and power up, or I'd be useless in a fight.

Just as I went to open the chest, I heard Pammy's voice in my head.

Attention Arizona Witches: this is your Sheriff. Do not be alarmed, but we have a state of emergency. Please be on the lookout for a large black metallic RV with heavy curtains and black rims. The witches navigating said vehicle are a danger to our way of life and hold a hostage. Do not approach. Contact me or any other soldier of fortune. Stay Vigilant.

Pammy's voice was gone, leaving behind a slight buzzing in my ears for a moment. Did she just mind-speak to the entire Arizona population of witches? I called my mother, who confirmed that she had heard the notice all the way down in Tucson. I got her off the phone quickly, not wanting to go into the detail when I really needed to take a nap. One thing was for certain, I hoped that Pammy was also getting a nap because if she didn't, she would be absolutely useless to everyone.

An hour later, I'd been fully invigorated and was ready to kick some ass. Unfortunately there had been no message to call in the cavalry yet. It struck me that by sending that message to all witches in a certain area, Pammy had also alerted our enemies. They'd already known that we'd been coming for them but now they knew we were on their tail.

I couldn't worry for Lola more than I already did, but I took the time to light a candle, asking the universe to help us find Lola and Yvette before it was too late. Like magic, my phone buzzed. I picked it up.

"We've got 'em. Think your friend Bruce would care to join the party?"

"I think he might be interested."

"I'll text the directions. Head over there, but do not approach until we have the entire group together."

I hung up and called Bruce, who was still holding down the fort at Lola's. I heard *Steel Magnolias* playing in the background and knew he'd done nothing but watch chick flicks since I last saw him. As I suspected, he was ready to rumble, sick of sitting on the sidelines. Normally a shifter wouldn't interfere in witch business, but Bruce was a close friend and exceptions were made given the right circumstances. The potential draining and murder of a close friend was one of those exceptions. I gave Bruce the instructions to the empty wash they'd been spotted in once again in East Mesa and the instructions not to approach until we were all in place. It was rather handy to have bear-shifting semi-immortal on our side.

I made it to the location in twenty minutes, making sure not to drive by the exact location in my very notice-able Jeep. Parking nearby in an empty warehouse district, I hopped out and jogged the quarter of a mile to where I saw Pammy's Crown Victoria. She and Dorothy were inside, and a moment later, I heard the rumble of Bruce's truck.

Pammy and Dorothy exited her vehicle as Bruce exited his own and joined us. I looked at our ragtag group of badasses but wondered if it'd be enough.

"Any chance we've got some more fortunes coming in for the fight?"

"You know we're always spread thin," Pammy said. "If, when we get there it looks like a suicide mission, we will pull back and call for citizen volunteers and for the others to start traveling in."

"Good enough for me," I said, ready to end this.

"Better than good enough for me," Bruce piped in. "It's been awhile since I've been in a magical brawl. Want me to change?" he asked.

Pammy shook her head. "This area is pretty deserted, but I really don't want animal control to be called with a sighting of a bear if we can help it. If things get dire, you're your own man and can decide what's best for the situation." In turn she looked at Dorothy and me. "That goes for you two as well. We stand up for the weak, and that is our job, but if a strategic retreat is necessary once we get in the fray, remember we can't kill them if we're dead."

"Let's do this thing," Dorothy piped in. "I've got to make some cupcakes for my son's class tomorrow."

Just like that, the tension that had been building dissipated as Pammy let out a hardy laugh. "I hope you save us all a cupcake."

"If you want to join me in frosting three dozen cupcakes, we can certainly come to an arrangement. Otherwise you're on your own, sister."

That only had Pammy laughing harder, and we all let out a chuckle to relieve the building tension, but the time had come. We walked into the wash. They'd hidden the RV behind some overgrown brush and tumbleweeds. It was a miracle that anyone had seen the vehicle at all.

"Peg, do a subtle feeler."

I pushed my magic out much like I'd done at the trailer park earlier, just in a small amount. There was a lot of magic happening in the trailer, dark inky magic that tried to climb on my own, but I gently pushed it back so as to not alert its spell-casters. Inside were four magic users. All of them felt wrong, and they were in the middle of something truly reprehensible.

"Four total, Pammy. Three of them are draining the fourth."

"We can handle three," Pammy said as she strode forward. She didn't knock. Her magic tore out of her ripping the door from its hinges. She went in, the rest of us climbing the metal stairs at her heels.

Three emaciated witches had turned their heads in a lizard-like fashion to stare at us. The effect was creepier because they were all on their hands and knees, circling the young woman whom I assumed to be Yvette. Her life force hung in the air to be consumed by these monsters.

"You did not come to my town and think you could get away with this, did you?" Pammy stared them down, hands on hips.

"Bitch, we get away with it everywhere." The male witch closest to us stood.

"Not this time. Peg, do the reversal," Pammy boomed into the small space.

I stepped to the side of Pammy and began my chant.

"*Life does not take life. Life nurtures life. Death does not live on but goes to its place. Death return to life what does not belong to you.*"

The three stood in unison, shocked looks on their faces. *Yep, that's right, cretins, we know the counter-curse.* They aimed their magic, but Dorothy, Bruce, and Pammy were on them, letting me complete my work.

I repeated the phrase over and over, all the while using my magic's energy to corral Yvette's life force. After my third recital, I pushed the last of the life force back into its owner. Yvette let out a death rattle, but her lungs started moving again. The three family members let out shrieks that were more animal than human causing my ears to ring.

I looked at the woman who stood farthest behind the prone form on the floor and saw her intention before she even realized it. She gathered her magic to force toward the unconscious woman. The old "if we can't have her no one will!" I ran the two steps and launched myself over Yvette, tackling the woman at the legs. She tumbled backward. We hit the floor and her spell went wild, hitting the ceiling in a burst of black sparks. The room went dark.

The air tasted musty and rancid at the same time. "What is it with you people and death spells for every gods-damn thing? If you're going to be monsters, maybe aim for some subtlety."

She laughed into the darkness. "I don't need subtle. You are nothing more than food to me." She tried to kick me off, but I crawled up her body like a monkey. I felt her magic gathering again, and I grabbed her head by her hair. She clawed at my hands, but I didn't give a damn as I slammed her head against the floor.

Even in the darkness I could see that she was momentarily dazed. Thank you, soldier of fortune boot camp. Witches really never did expect you to go for plain old physical damage when magic was on the table. She shook her head and began to claw again with renewed effort. So, I slammed her head against the floor again and again until she lay still. I reached out with my magic. She was still alive, but she wouldn't be moving for a while.

I turned to my friends. Bruce was in a grappling pose with one of the witches, but he looked to have it under control. Pammy and Dorothy were another story. Even though it was two against one, the male witch was throwing everything he had at them. Black sparks kept erupting in the room. It was difficult to see. The man wasn't trying to knock anyone out. He was fighting to the death. I looked down at Yvette, still out and in the middle of it.

I looked around and saw a nook in between two bench seats where a fold-up table could go. It was better than where she lay sprawled in the middle of the RV, so I ran over to her, gripping her under her armpits and dragged her into the space.

Now, that she was relatively out of harm's way, I turned back to Pammy and Dorothy. Dorothy was on the floor. My heart jumped to my throat. Anger surged forward, bringing with it a shocking amount of power that made my skin vibrate. The witch battling Pammy turned to me, the power too tempting a meal to ignore.

"She needs to make cupcakes, you asshole!" I screamed as I let go the power that now sizzled at my skin. It burst from me, hitting him straight in the chest and just kept punching as he backed away from the force. Frantically, he tried to raise his hands to send some magic my way, but he couldn't get them up. He let out a strangled scream and crumpled to the floor.

I wanted to stop then, but it was like all of the anger and helplessness I'd experienced the last few days stopped me from reining myself in. Sweat fell down my forehead at the strain it took to maintain this much power. My teeth clenched as I tried to let go. Hands fell on my shoulders, and I almost directed my power toward whoever held me but then she spoke.

"Let go, Sug, they're not worth your power, especially when I've got this here knife. A twist in the heart, and he'll never hurt another person."

My magic dropped away instantly as I realized what she was trying to tell me. My anger had taken control. I'd been perilously low on magic. My body shuddered in revulsion at the thought of literally draining myself.

"There now, this here is a mobile den of evil, and their dark magic has permeated every nook and cranny. Under normal circumstances, your body would have shut it down much earlier."

I shivered involuntary. "Is Dorothy okay?" I asked through chattering teeth.

"She fell when avoiding one of those bastards' curses. Knocked herself out good. I think I'm going to need to spring for some bakery cupcakes for her."

"Yeah."

The third and final witch flew past us and into the wall. Bruce was right behind him, looking more fearsome than I'd ever seen the generally happy-go-lucky man.

Pammy held up her hand to stop Bruce. "We only need one." She marched over to the dazed man, pulled out a large hunting knife with a black blade, and before I could do so much as squeak, stabbed the man in the chest, twisted, and then slit his throat. She stepped over his body and moved swiftly to the other man I'd pushed back with my magic and efficiently did the same. "The Arizona sheriff has judged you and found you both guilty of our highest sin. May your afterlife be filled with torment."

I just stared at Pammy, never having witnessed a judgment before.

She looked back at me eyes steady. "Normally, you say that part before you kill them, but if they're truly dangerous, feel free to bend the rules."

"Sure," I agreed, only capable of one-syllable answers at the moment.

"I think our Peggy girl is in a bit of shock."

Pammy looked over at Bruce. "Don't call her Peggy when she's in no condition to yell at you. Lay her on that bench seat next to the victim, Dorothy on the other. They could do with some healing, but first we need to bind the third witch. I want to question her before I kill her."

I wanted to argue that I was fine, but Bruce had already scooped me up in his arms, and I realized then how close I'd been to falling flat on my face. The moment I reclined, I knew I couldn't stand up again of my own will. While I analyzed my own predicament, Dorothy was deposited on the opposite bench, facing me.

"We're bad ass," I mumbled.

I took her responding grunt as an agreement.

"You two comfortable?" Pammy called at us.

"Yes," I mumbled.

"Good, now, I don't believe you've ever been in the presence of a binding spell, Peg. These things can be— uncomfortable. Dorothy you know the drill."

The chanting began, and magic filled the room. If by uncomfortable she'd meant it felt like my magic had clawed its way as far inside myself as possible—like a thousand little needles to your skin, then, yes, I'd say that it was uncomfortable. Magic didn't want to be bound.

After some time had passed, the chanting stopped, and all that was left was a buzzing on my skin that didn't seem to want to go away. Pammy's face loomed over mine.

"All right, ladies, she's bound up like a Christmas goose. Now, I have just enough juice left to give you two a little health back. The way I figure it, two witches on their feet are better than one old crone, but I'm going to need you two to handle the bodies if I do this. Is this something you two will be able to do?"

"Yes," Dorothy croaked.

"Peg?" Pammy's umber skin had a sheen of perspiration on it, and fine lines that I'd never really noticed stood out. The realization hit that she was just as wiped as both of us, and she didn't really have the energy to do what she offered.

I really wished that I could just go be put in George for an hour, but even though Pammy had it all figured out, there wasn't time for that. The plane lore came back to me in detail. The goblins used it as a power source. No matter where they were, they could call on the wealth they'd hidden there. Being only part goblin, I didn't require the wealth portion, only the magical realm. How did they access it?

"Just give me a few minutes, Pammy," I mumbled.

My magic was already buried deep inside of me. Convenient that I needed it there to search the innermost places of my soul. I put myself into a trance, the buzzing on my skin helped keep me from falling into the other side of wakefulness. At first, I just searched within myself, finding nothing I hadn't sensed before in my own soul. A minute passed, and I knew soon Pammy would just pelt me with a healing spell even though she didn't have the juice.

Something clicked, and I remembered that George was not intrinsically part of me. He was his own being that had chosen to bond with me. With that, I called out in my mind's eye for him. Almost immediately, he appeared, and a door opened in my magic's soul.

Energy, a warm, light lavender like the sky of George covered my vision. The buzzing on my skin became a comforting magical tingle. The magic kept filling me, reviving me. Once I felt like I could no longer hold any more, I gently closed the door, thanking George, who sent one final warm zing along our bond.

I sat straight up, and Pammy took a startled step back, looking me over. "What in the world?"

"You have your secrets; I have mine."

She gave me a hard stare. "I can guess at yours."

"You can, and you may be right, but I'd prefer if you'd let me tell you in my own time."

She thought about it for a moment and gave me a nod.

I stood, my legs no longer shaky. I felt as if I could run a marathon. I looked around at the people present. The sheen of sweat and wrinkles prominent on Pammy's face hid the unhealthy gray tone to her skin. Then I looked to Dorothy.

"Is she passed out?"

"Yup, too much strain along with the concussion." Pammy's voice had tremor to it that she'd managed to almost hide.

"Should we be letting her sleep with a concussion?"

"Figured she'd be fine given that I'll be hitting her with some healing in under five minutes."

"Uh, yeah, I think you should leave the healing to me, starting with yourself. You're exhausted."

Her mouth turned into a hard line. "My witches come first."

"Pammy, you're our strongest magical warrior. It's only a matter of time before the rest of their group show up. I want you healthy, first, to watch my back, and we don't have the time to argue about this." I thrust my hand forward, placing my hand over her heart.

Magic poured out, not so much a healing spell since I saw no signs of injuries other than bruises and a few scratches. Her current issue was magical depletion. Pammy used what little energy she had to give me a hard glare that even a week ago I would have cowered at. Instead I tilted my chin, looking down at her with my best "whatcha gonna do about it" look. She shook her head in annoyance, but then I felt a shift in her magic. Pammy had shields on shields on shields. Her magic moved in a way that almost felt mechanical, like a vault opening one lever at a time. A tiny crack opened, and my power flooded her. Startled, she took a step back but then stood straight as the warm undertones returned to her skin.

Any moment now, she'd have teetered over, and Bruce would have been stuck carrying four witches. After a few minutes, Pammy's hand came up to grip my wrist, signaling that she was good. She turned to help Dorothy, but I stopped her with a hand on her shoulder. My energy levels were still crazy high, and I didn't want Pammy to drain herself again. Dorothy was still out, which made her more receptive to my healing.

My hand again over her heart, I began to push my energy into her. This time, however, I also recited a small healing spell to counteract the bump and accompanying concussion. She began to stir but didn't remove my hand as she sat up slowly. After a few minutes, it was Pammy who pulled me back.

"Let's not drain you, my dear."

I wanted to argue because I could just ask George to

open the door once more, but she was right, and on second thought, I should really ask Deval or even Delmy or Griselda if there were limits or rules. I didn't want to mistakenly hurt the plane that so kindly offered up a magical boost along with a safe haven. Dorothy stood up with a slight wobble, but she was standing. She looked over at me with cautious eyes.

"Thanks for the boost."

"No problem."

"Now, Dorothy, this is one of those need-to-know things. I trust you to keep this to yourself."

Dorothy looked between us for a moment. "Not sure what exactly I'm keeping to myself, but of course I will."

I got the impression that Dorothy had been told to keep a lot of things to herself over the years, and since Pammy hadn't hunted her down yet for betrayal, that was good enough for me.

"Should we wake up Yvette?" I asked, concerned about the witch that still lay on the ground.

Pammy reached down and felt the woman's pulse. "No, our little miss here is going to need some specialized care, being almost drained, and she'll be going into withdrawals as well. I want her in a safe house before that starts. Pulse is good, and the magic has pulled itself in tight. Poor little bird is traumatized but not in any current danger. Besides, she probably wouldn't enjoy watching us dispose of the bodies."

"Why? Aren't we just going to call BBTT?"

"Nope, Sug, too much dark magic can wreak all sorts of chaos on a corpse. We need to burn the bodies, preferably while our evil sleeping beauty watches, so she'll give us some information."

"I need to call my husband to tell him I'll be late." Dorothy accepted Pammy's statement just like that. "Did I hear you mention in my semi-unconscious state that you'd foot the bill for some cupcakes?"

"Course I will. Call the Hemlock Bakery and have them bill it to me. It's near your home, right?"

"Yes, ma'am. I'll have John pick them up. I just need to pop over to the car to get my phone," she said as she walked to the exit.

"You ladies sure know how to show an old bear an exciting time."

I jumped a little; he'd been so quiet up until now. I looked over, and he sat on the built-in couch along the wall. One of the drainers lay at his feet, the blood from the heart-stabbing and throat-slitting seeping into the carpet.

Bruce stood and opened the door for Dorothy. "Care for a tagalong? I figure we'll want to use my truck for transport, and I don't think any of us should wander off alone in this area."

"Take him with you, Dorothy," Pammy ordered.

"Sheesh, woman, I was planning on it."

"Sorry, been hanging out with this one too much lately." She pointed her thumb at me.

"Are you indicating that I'm a problem child?" I deadpanned.

"Not indicating it, stating it. Now shoo, you two, we've got hours of work left for us before this night is over."

19

It was always helpful to have a friend with a truck when you needed to dispose of bodies. Sure, they would have fit in the back of my Jeep, but I'd rather clean off blood with a hose than a scrub brush and upholstery cleaner. Pammy put the live one, still unconscious from when I'd bounced her head like a basketball on the floor, in the trunk of her car just in case the woman had some tricks up her sleeve when she woke. Bodies loaded, we searched the trailer.

The trailer had plenty of damning magical literature, which included various tomes on the art of the sacrifice. The ages varied with some so old the bindings were cracking to more modern spiral-bound notebooks. At a quick glance, they appeared to be in the same handwriting, but we could look at that more closely later. Pammy was always prepared and pulled a few empty file boxes out of her trunk before we stuck the witch in it. Pammy set the wards she had on her trunk, making me wish I had a trunk to set magical locks in.

We filled all three-binder boxes to overflowing and did

a final search before Pammy started the first fire of the night. Her magic was an inferno contained to the expensive RV, not touching any of the dry brush that surrounded it.

While the fire raged, I stood next to Pammy, my hand on her shoulder as a focus while her arms outstretched, controlled the most volatile element. It burned on and on, its smoke trapped in a magical field so as to not alert the neighbors. They could still see it if they drove by, but the vehicle itself had oozed with malevolent magic and needed to be destroyed. The heat stuck inside burned hotter and hotter until all that was left was charred metal. Pammy closed her outstretched palms into fists, reversing her arms and pulling her elbows straight back. The flames winked out, and the field broke, bringing the smell of charred rubber and ozone.

We turned to walk back to our vehicles. Bruce and Dorothy already sat in their cars, ready to get the show, or body disposal, on the road.

As we approached, I couldn't help but wonder out loud. "Why didn't we just burn the witches along with the RV?"

Pammy didn't stop her forward stride. "Right now, it's an old RV that got burnt up by some delinquents. No one is going to report it missing, and I doubt that the McAllisters have a direct tie to the title on the vehicle, but if we were to leave some charred bodies behind, we'd need to deal with the human authorities."

"Why would that matter? We police our own."

"We do, but then there's paperwork. Who were these witches? How did they die? If it was an execution, I need to justify it. I need to pay for disposal. Yada yada yada. Besides bones carry magic, so we're taking them to a designated site to burn and dispose of them where we will then salt the earth, so no blundering police officer can take a witch's bone home as a trophy to show his kids only to have weird shit start happening in his house with the cop blaming it on us."

"Has that really happened?"

"It has. Now, get your ass in your car. Try to keep up, grandma."

"Yeah, yeah."

I jogged back to my Jeep, and we pulled away from the wash that now had a crispy RV to add to the ambiance of brush, tumbleweeds, and mesquite trees. Pammy pulled out first, followed by Bruce and then Dorothy. I took up the rear, so I'd have plenty of time to see the various turns made by the three cars in front of me. Pammy was kind and kept her speeding to a minimum. It likely had more to do with her having a witch in her trunk and less to do with me being at the rear of our caravan. We drove for over an hour, heading east into what I'd thought was state park land. The last half an hour was all dirt roads, making me bounce along in my Jeep. I cringed thinking of Dorothy in her little compact car.

We came to a stop in a small valley between two rocky hills covered in cholla cactus, known to some as jumping cactus, but I liked to kept simple and call it Satan's plant. Unlike its surrounding landscape, the small valley didn't have any rocks or gravel in it, just dirt. Rocks could absorb magic, so this area had been cleared. To the far right of the area sat a large woodpile. Knowing what this place was for gave me the heebie-jeebies. Two of the witches we were disposing of were already dead, but burning, hanging, crushing, or drowning were all triggers for a witch with any sense.

"Peg, get out of your car and go start gathering wood. Take it to the center of the field."

I hopped out and went about doing Pammy's bidding. When I grabbed the dried-out mesquite wood, a small bite of magic startled me. I looked harder at the wood and saw that it was emitting a soft white glow. *Purification magic*. Dorothy helped me gather the wood while Pammy took the pieces, creating an intricate design out of them. Bruce carried over the two bodies, and Pammy had him lay them in the center of the patterned circle, one on top of the other in a cross pattern.

"All right, girls and boy, we are four here tonight, so let's do this right. Bruce you have any objections to joining a witch's circle?"

"No, ma'am, I live for the excitement of it all."

"You take the west, Peg take the south, Dorothy the east, and I'll grab the north. I'll do the chant. Hum along once you get the rhythm. Dorothy you know the chant, so feel free join once you have the cadence down. Peg, try and listen to the words. This is a good learning opportunity."

"All very Magic School Bus," I responded.

"Smart ass."

I grinned at her. I couldn't help it when I thought of this as a weird-ass, macabre study session.

"Bruce, will you help me grab the crazy bitch in my trunk?"

"Like I said, the excitement of it all."

They brought back the woman, who was still unconscious. It was the first chance I'd had to really look at her. Even when I'd been banging her head against the floor, I'd been in a frenzy for survival and hadn't studied her; I did now. The woman looked to be in her seventies, at least, though her strength earlier would suggest otherwise. Her skin, wrinkled and loose, hung off her bones, so gray she looked like a corpse. The dark circles and thinning dishwater-blond hair that hung in lank pieces made it possible to see her age-spotted scalp. I shuddered.

"You going to wake her up?" Dorothy asked Pammy.

"Yup, these people are cold hearted, but I'm hoping that some purified fire may make her tongue looser."

"She has to know she's going to die. Why would the fire matter to her?" I asked, questioning Pammy's reasoning.

"She knows she's gonna die, but is she gonna die quick like her friends, or are we going to throw her on top of their bodies to burn alive?" she asked.

Revulsion crawled along my skin. "Would you really do that?"

"Don't have pity for her, Peg. She's a walking blight on our people, and she would burn you alive in an instant."

"Does that make it better?"

Pammy sighed. "I'm going to try and avoid it, Peg, but if she doesn't answer our questions, I will do it. I never want to see this family or another like it near my territory again."

Just like that, our hard-as-nails, relentless, fearless leader returned. The shiver that ran down my spine competed with the warm fuzzy feeling I had knowing Pammy would do whatever she had to do to protect me. Pammy stepped past me to the unconscious woman. For a moment, I thought she was going to kick the woman awake, but instead she reached down and sent a sharp zap of electricity into her prone form. I winced, having been on the end of one of those during childhood fights with my sister that had gone too far. The juxtaposition of childhood versus adult games was not lost on me.

The nameless woman went from the fetal position to sitting up in one swift movement. It looked odd and possibly against the laws of physics with her hands tied behind her back. She stared around at all of us and literally hissed, baring her teeth, before speaking in a low guttural language that made my skin crawl and had me wanting to take a step back.

Pammy just laughed. "Do you really believe I would be so stupid as to not bind your powers? You're in Arizona, bitch, and you belong to me to live or to die as I choose."

The woman spat at Pammy, managing to land some spittle on her boot. "I belong to no one. Death does not scare me, and you do not have the power to hold me forever."

"I don't need forever." Pammy walked behind the woman, grabbed her harshly by the shoulders, and forced her to face the pyre that contained her comrades. "If you weren't scared of death then why feed on the living? Your friends here have already paid the price. What price do you think I'll make you pay?"

"You are too weak," she stated, clearly looking into the dusk. "There was no torture. You killed them true and clean. You want answers from me, but my family will come for me. I won't be so kind."

"Keen observations. You're right. Their deaths were quick, a mercy really, but I have no doubt you've been alive years longer than I due to your atrocious feeding habits, so you must know by now that the weak often pay for the mistakes of others. Peg, over here, knocked you out by physical means not magical ones, how embarrassing for you. Since you were so easy to put down, I have no doubt that you will give me the answers I seek because you wouldn't be able to handle real pain. Them." She gestured toward the two bodies. "They probably could have handled it. You have two simple choices. Talk, I'll kill you quick. Don't talk, and I'll make a new pyre, special, just for you. Olden time justice. European tradition never goes out of style."

The woman snarled again, but I could see the rising panic in her sunken eyes.

"Well, then, let's do a demo, shall we? We'll burn your friends. The scent of burning flesh is, well, oddly terrifying. Maybe you know this, but have you ever been to a luau?" Pammy paused waiting for an answer she didn't get. "Burning humans smell a lot like a roasted pig. Brings up all kinds of uncomfortable thoughts for normal people. Then again, you feed on witches, so maybe it won't bother you at all."

"We feed on magic, you sick fuck. We're not cannibals."

Pammy started laughing again. "You really see a difference? They're one and the same. You're blind devotion to your family could be described as naïve, but in reality it is willful stupidity. Put someone on a spit covered in pineapples or consume the very essence of their being, these are not different where it matters. The only difference is the special effects, for one would earn and R rating if it were a film the other PG or PG-13." Pammy clapped once turning away from the woman. "Places people."

I hurried to my spot, trying to shake the visual image of a charred human covered in pineapple. More like NC-17. Her chant began as soon as we all stood in our assigned corners. I stretched my hands out to the east and west, allowing my power to flow through to Dorothy and Bruce, who did the same, connecting me with Pammy as well.

Shifters weren't able to throw about magic like witches, so he didn't have a visible stream of magic coming from him like the other two, but he was magic, and he was pushing that persona out toward us, primal, animalistic, raw with nature. It was the first time that I'd personally felt his magic in action, and the power of it almost biting.

Forcing my attention away from Bruce, I focused on

Pammy. It didn't take long to find the rhythm of her chant, the melodic harmony that she requested we all join. I hummed along, trying to decipher the words but failing despite Pammy's earlier instructions. I'd need to ask for a transcript later, but for now, all I could focus on was the growing power and the heat. A fireball burst in the middle of the pyre, so hot I could see blue flames among the orange in the ten-foot fire. My face burned from being so close, but I didn't drop the chant, didn't lose the melody.

The song continued on until there was nothing left but gray ash and bone shards. Pammy stopped the chant, dropping her hands in the same instant before she turned and marched back to the hostage. I dropped my own arms, which ached, and followed Pammy back. I walked up and heard Pammy once again interrogating the woman. I couldn't reach Pammy levels of deprivation in my threats, so I just stood behind her and tried to look menacing. It wasn't hard given all of the havoc and pain these witches had caused over the last few days.

"Now, as you can see, I have plenty of firewood left. The only difference this time is that an awful soprano of your screams will be added to my song. Well, you would add to it until your vocal cords burned. Pity that, but I'll know that you will still be there screaming silently, suffering horribly. Do you think it will take you longer to die given all of the life forces you've stolen over the years?"

The woman looked up, her eyes meeting Pammy's. Moments before they had been hateful but flat. A gaze one acquired from witnessing or performing unthinkable deeds. Now they almost glowed. "I've lived longer than you, hag, and I will not betray those that have given me the blessing of allowing me to live as our true nature demands. Burn me. It will be a fitting end to a life lived dedicated to a higher glory." The woman spit at Pammy, barely missing her shoe this time. *Being bound really limited your physical reaction options.*

Pammy sighed and kicked some dirt over the spittle. "Zealots, you can never reason with them." She looked back over her shoulder at the three of us. "A threat that is not followed through on is a weakness." Still looking over her shoulder at us, she lifted her arm. The woman was flung on top of the ash that remained of her cohorts. Wood from the pile followed, flying through the air to land on top of the woman. Her earlier silence ended as she shrieked, her current reality finally catching up with her.

The disassociation I'd experienced during the corpse bonfire unfortunately disappeared just in time to allow me to witness one of my greatest fears. Pammy turned her head and looked at the witch now partly covered in wood.

"Any last words?"

More shrieking was her only answer. Pammy didn't ask that a circle be performed this time. She began her chant again. Power radiated off of her as the words were said with more authority than they had been before. In her song, I heard the bleakness that came with being the ultimate authority. The loneliness that went hand-in-hand with power. I wanted to be strong for her, to place a hand on her shoulder, so she knew that I recognized the sacrifices she made for all of us, but where the screams had brought on nausea, the smell, just as Pammy had described it, sent what little self-control I had out the window. It had been there before with the corpses but knowing the smell was coming from a live person was too much.

I ran from our group and retched everything from my stomach behind a tumbleweed. Behind me, the shrieks had ended, leaving only the sound of a roaring fire and the smell of burnt flesh. The realization had me dry heaving all over again. The chant ended, and I felt a hand on my back.

"It had to be done," Pammy's husky voice whispered to me.

Hands on my knees, I took a deep breath in through my mouth, trying to ignore the smell and straightened. I looked Pammy in the eyes. "I know it did. I'll always be grateful for what you are willing to do to protect us."

There was a shimmer in Pammy's eyes, but she turned away. "Glad to hear it. Can't blame you for ralphing. It's not a pleasant experience, especially not your first time." She turned and walked back toward the others, and I followed her. "Okay, people, we need to bury the fire pit. I'd like to say that we accomplished a lot today, but these people were only zealot followers of the true powers, so there will be more work to be done..." Lights caught our eyes from off in the distance. Blue flashing lights. "Hold that thought, you three. Now we're on our land, performing witch business, but I'd rather the humans not catch a whiff of this one. So, scatter, I will take care of this."

"Pammy, you must be drained. I can help," I protested.

"I said scatter, and I meant it. Take separate routes. If anyone stops you, you were going for an evening hike, and you got a bit turned around before finding your car. Now get."

When Pammy told me to get, I got. Back at the cars, we agreed that Bruce and I would take more creative roads home given our all-terrain vehicles. Dorothy would likely be stopped on her way down, but her whole mom vibe would likely end whatever suspicion was aimed at her. I bit my lip thinking about Pammy being left alone, but now I knew, more than ever, that whatever came Pammy's way would either make nice or suffer the consequences.

20

————

Driving through dried-out brush and washes while trying to avoid large rocks with minimal use of headlights did not top the list of my skill set. I thought I'd made it about a mile down the road before I realized that I would die on this mountain if I kept going. So, I pulled off the pathetic trail of a service road I'd stumbled onto behind some spindly tree that would not provide much coverage if a flashlight was involved. Desert plants were not great at hiding people on the run.

I sat there in the darkness, the only light coming from a hazy cloud-shrouded moon and the dim blue of the lights that still danced below me, further down the mountain where they'd stopped to pay Pammy a visit. The quiet of the desert felt unnerving. The soft hoot of an owl had me jumping out of my seat, that and my phone suddenly coming to life with the Josie and the Pussycats theme song nearly caused my heart to stop. Partly because it had been so long since I'd heard the campy song, my joke at Lola's resemblance to the cartoon character that played Melody, partly because the quiet it erupted from.

I scrambled to grab the phone, which made me an instant klutz, as I knocked it off of the passenger seat. Lunging over the mid console, I managed to grab it about one second before it would have gone to voicemail and answered.

"Hello?" I stage whispered into the phone in deference to the quiet that surrounded me.

"Peg!" Lola practically shrieked. Excitement coated her voice.

"Lola, where are you? I've been so worried about you. Are you all right?"

"Let's not start this again, Peg. I just needed to get away for a while, but I have really exciting news! Michael and I are eloping! Can you believe it?"

My stomach felt like a lead weight had been dropped in it. "Where are you, Lola?"

Static on the phone line was all I heard. I looked at my phone screen. There was only one bar available, and it was barely hanging on for life. I pushed it back up to my ear.

"Lola, I'm having a hard time hearing you."

Through the static came a reply, "Maid…honor… chapel….here…. soon."

"Can you repeat that?"

The static cleared, and I heard a woman the background. "Who are you talking to, you naughty girl?" The tone tried for benevolent, but I heard the underlying anger. Lola didn't.

"Don't be upset. I had to tell her. She's my maid of honor." Then she giggled.

"Well, dear, let me say 'hello' then." Lola must have passed the phone because suddenly I heard the words whispered that I never wanted to hear. "You're too late." The call disconnected.

I held my phone for a moment, staring at it. Below me,

the blue lights still flared hazily in the night. I needed to get off of the mountain, but I also needed to do so without a police chase. I dialed Pammy's number, hoping that she'd picked up, and that little service bar hung on for dear life. Lady luck finally smiled at me.

"Little busy now, Sug."

"Lola called."

"How interesting."

"She says she eloping, but another woman came on the phone saying we were too late, so I'm guessing there's a little extra ceremony to this ceremony, if you know what I mean."

"I do know what you mean."

I gripped my steering wheel and wanted to scream. "I can't get off the mountain without the cops chasing me. Can you keep them with you somehow or cause a distraction, so I can get down the main road without driving off the mountain?"

"I can do that. Have a good time, dear. Make sure you get some friends to go along with you."

I set my phone down and turned on my lights, making my way back to the service trail and finally back to the main dirt road. My old Jeep was not quiet, but at no point did I hear approaching sirens, so Pammy had been able to keep the cops busy. My bounce down the mountain made it too difficult to make any calls for help. All I could do was replay Lola's words over and over in my head.

She wanted a maid of honor, which meant that they were keeping up the farce of a wedding as a cover for some other ceremony. They could have just gotten her a white dress from Dillard's and currently been in someone's back-yard with a guy named Phil who'd gotten ordained through some fifteen-minute online course that cost fifty bucks. Or was it all real and they were trying to get her to marry in as a recruitment for a new initiate? They were currently down three members, but did they know that?

Then I remembered. She'd said chapel. Phoenix was no Vegas, and there weren't a lot of "chapels" to choose from, and only one that I knew that Lola both knew of and loved. An antique home near downtown Mesa that had been a farmhouse in an earlier life. Now painted white with green shutters and a white picket fence, trellis roses, and ivy climbing its walls, the Vintage Wedding House was popular for brides looking for an intimate romantic affair with a smaller guest list.

I hoped the chapel didn't have a secret side business in dark magical sacrifices, but either way I needed to commit to a location. Going with your gut is always better than sitting around with your thumb up your ass, so I pressed the gas a little more, ignoring the minor fishtailing the back of my Jeep performed as my tires skidded along some gravel. What was an axle compared to a best friend?

My tires finally hit asphalt, and I pressed the gas pedal down further. This far into the mountains, I didn't think that I'd run into a deputy at night, particularly given that nearby local officials were all preoccupied with Pammy. I had no qualms with engaging in a high-speed chase if necessary.

Even with the pavement as an indicator that I'd returned to the modern civilization, my cell service was spotty at best. So, I recklessly drove in barely lit streets while fumbling with my phone. Pammy, I already knew, was occupied, but I still called and left a voicemail to tell her where I was going. I tried calling Bruce after that, and the call went straight to voicemail. I figured he was still high up in the mountains playing possum. Dorothy and I had yet to exchange numbers, so that was a dead end.

My last call was to outside help, and one of the gods,

demi-gods, entities, or spirits finally deigned to answer my prayers. Deval picked up on the third ring, just as I nearly skidded out turning on to the US 60, leaving behind the smell of burnt rubber and ozone.

"Yes?"

"Are you busy?" A sudden realization hit me. In my panic, I'd briefly forgotten that Lola was a goblin citizen. "Actually, I don't care if you're busy. Lola is about to be sacrificed, and I need some backup. You do claim her right?"

Deval growled into the phone. "You know that we claim her. Tell me everything."

I went over everything I knew, including our earlier culling of the rogue witch herd and where I suspected the ceremony would be held.

"That seems a little odd. Why not just kill her in the desert somewhere? Why bother with this drawn out facade of marriage and companionship? It does not make sense, especially to go the trouble to actually reserve a venue for a murder ceremony."

I thought about t for a moment. "It may be part of their ritual. A happy victim gives a better pay off? If that's the case, and they've been living off of the bite junkies, Lola will be Kobe beef compared to canned Spam. Or maybe they want her to join the family. I'm going in blind."

"You think this is the case?"

"Fuck if I know. I'm guessing at this point, Deval. All I know is that my friend is in trouble. Are you willing to go against a coven of uber-dark witches?"

"It is my duty. I will see if I can gather others."

"I'll be there in thirty minutes." I willed my car to go faster.

"It looks as though I will beat you there. Is Pammy available to attend the wedding?"

"She's currently disposing of dead witches and holding off the Maricopa County sheriffs. She might make the reception."

"I will see you there. Be safe."

21

My foot pressed the gas peddle as far as it would go, and it still felt like I was driving at a snail's pace. The entire drive there, my heart pounded with anxiety of either being pulled over and being too late to save my friend or just being too late, period. Frustration had tears stinging at my eyes. I blinked them back. I'd be no good to Lola if I showed up as an emotional wreck, unable to help her once I got there.

I slowed my demon's pace after exiting the freeway. Downtown Mesa had a low speed limit and a high police presence given that their headquarters were just around the block. I drove by the vintage house, and sure enough, I saw hints of candlelight along with magic. Magical beings would recognize the light, colorful hues that played through the lace curtains as magic, but the average human wouldn't be able to see it.

Full-blown witch with some goblin mixed in, I saw the magic and felt the malevolence of it. I considered scoping the house out, making the smart entrance, but then I saw a luxury black sedan that screamed Deval, and I knew he was already inside. So, I parked and quickly sprinted to the house, even managing a slightly less than graceful hurdle over the decorative picket fence to avoid wasting time opening it. The front screen of the little white farmhouse had climbing roses and ivy running up trellises on either side. I slammed the door open, silently apologizing to the blooms I no doubt smashed in the process.

The scene before me left little time to worry about flowers. The front room of the home had been converted to a chapel. A haze of dark magic hovered about the pulpit area, much like we'd seen in the witches' trailer. Deval and Vegard blocked the aisle while fighting off two dark practitioners. The witches, like their brethren we'd run into earlier, looked emaciated and haggard and should have been no problem for Deval and Vegard, but dark magic was often accompanied by a sly strength.

Watching the witches throw spell after spell at my who-knew-what, and his cousin, made me realize how lucky we'd been at the trailer. I jumped to Deval's right and threw up my arms, letting my magic fly at a particularly nasty magic spell that had come his way. The black spell crawled up my own green magical aura for a moment, which left me slightly panicked before it fizzled out. I blinked and remembered the vaccine I'd taken at Deval's public condo. Thank gods, I needed all of the help I could get. A hiss escaped the man who'd sent the spell my way.

"Good of you to be so prompt," Deval called to me. "I believe the bride wishes to see you. We can handle the groom's guests."

I nodded and jumped into a pew, climbing over the seats to avoid Deval, his cousin, and the two McCallisters fighting in the aisle. One reached out to touch me, and I barely managed a quick dodge. His hands were coated with black magic, and I really didn't have the time to find out what nasty little spell he wanted to infect me with. As I scrambled over the pews, I saw that another group of the dark witches surrounded Lola. She was lying in the middle of a witch's circle as they held hands and chanted. Lola was decked out in a fifties-style white A-line dress with a small veil on her head. She didn't appear to be conscious from a distance and her prone form gave off a vibe of a bespelled princess waiting to awaken.

I wasn't her prince charming: I was better. I was her gods-damned best friend, and that meant no one got to fuck with her but me. I ran forward and did what any highly trained professional who'd recently undergone advanced training did. I plowed into the circle like I was playing Red Rover. I broke the first set of hands and leaped over Lola to break another set. The witches looked up in shock. I did a quick turn to face them, throwing my palms up, adrenaline and my power answering to surge my magic forward. "Maid of honor, reporting for duty!" I called out giving them what I hoped was a maniacal grin. You had to be crazy to take on these odds.

Michael took a step forward, stepping on the skirt of Lola's dress. A woman sharply dressed in a skirt suit and heels of all things placed a hand on his chest, pushing him back. She looked to be in her early forties. She had frosted blonde hair done up in an elegant twist and was wearing tasteful makeup. The sick bitch had dressed like she actually planned to see her son wed and not murder my best friend.

"You must be mommy dearest."

She smiled at me, looking me over as if I were a fly caught in her web. I might be, but I wouldn't let Lola die without trying to save her.

"I've heard of you. Peg, is it?" She sniffed the air, her

smile growing even more perverse. "And a mongrel, too. Michael, you didn't tell me you had found a mutt."

Michael's eyebrows drew together and he sniffed the air, mimicking his mother. "I'm sorry, Mother. She's always been in the presence of goblins. I didn't notice the distinction."

She reached up and patted his cheek. "It's of no matter, but what a wonderful treat for us."

Goody, my odd family line was considered a delicacy to these psychos. I looked at the other two people that made up the circle of four. Unlike Michael and the head bitch in charge, they took on the emaciated androgynous look of their other brethren.

"You gonna share? I don't mean to question your management style, but this all feels very 'Let them eat cake.' So you have these lackeys that you turn from witches into creatures more vile than vampires, and then you have them do your bidding, jonesing for that sweet, sweet life force all while you and your son here take the best pickings?"

She laughed. It was a high-pitched tinkle of a laugh that made me want to punch her in the face.;

"Do you think to turn my family against me? We always survive—"

"Tell that to your buddies at the trailer."

Her eyes darkened and she literally hissed at me like the serpent she was. "I felt them leave. Are you saying you are the one who harmed our family?"

"I mean I can't take all of the credit. It was a group effort. You've really pissed off Pammy, and frankly that alone should be enough to have you running for the hills or sewer; ya know, wherever you feel most comfortable."

"You are such a child."

"Madam, why are we speaking to this one?" one of the minions piped up.

"Jeffrey, don't interrupt me. It's been a long time since I've seen one of her kind. You do remember, don't you? We had one with connections once. We feasted on her for years."

"Connections?" I asked before I could stop myself.

"Of course. Do you think that we, having lived centuries, would not know of the planes? We can't, of course, steal the goblin magic. It is but a cousin to our own powers, but mixed with a witch's blood, it makes for a quite powerful meal. A mule, if you will, with the smooth ride of a horse but the stamina of a jackass."

My mouth dropped open. "I'm not sure if I'm more put off by you discussing what a fine meal I'd make or because you just compared your feeding habits to animal husbandry."

She waved a hand. "It's of no matter. My family will feast tonight, and we will all regain our youth. Then we will, as you so aptly put it, run for the hills, not the sewer. We are not a confrontational type, so we will leave your sheriff in peace, and she will forget us once we've moved on. They always do."

I glanced back behind them and saw that during our little interlude, Deval and Vegard had managed to knock out one of the witches they'd been fighting, but they looked tired. I tried not to worry. I was sure they had plenty of gold to pull from.

"Yeah, but you do know who that goblin back there is right?" I said, pointing out Deval.

She didn't even bother to look back. "The affairs of goblins do not concern me as long as they keep to their kind. They will die tonight and be nothing but an afterthought."

"Yeah, about that. That's Deval, the crown prince of the Arizona goblins. I know you mentioned hiding out between your little parasitic vacations, but you may have heard of his mother, Delmy. Now, I've met her, and let me tell you, one scary lady, and she really does love that boy. Also, you know that whole immortal thing. She won't think twice about spending decades, centuries even, tracking you down to watch you burn."

I finally saw a small crack in the matriarch's face. The smile that she'd held this entire time twitched. She knew I was right. She herself appeared to be a doting mother to a single boy. Mama's boys weren't nearly as scary as their mamas.

"It matters not, Mother. We have invested too much of our power in Lola. If that goblin chose to interfere, it's his own undoing, and we will be gone before she feels the death collapse of her son's plane."

She nodded once, broken from her introspection. "You're right of course, my darling boy."

Our chat had come to an end. I let loose the power I'd been building, hitting her and Michael in one jolt. They took a step back. Even with the element of surprise there were four witches juiced up on death magic. Dark magic began to coalesce around me, and I had nowhere to run.

"Don't spell her. We will feast on her as well as her friend," Mommy dearest screeched.

The dark magic made a hasty retreat and was replaced by fists and feet as I was struck over and over. I held my own despite being pummeled. I knocked my head back and felt the satisfaction of cartilage breaking in a nose. I kicked and punched and clawed in my determination to save my friend. But then a sharp pain hit the back of my head, and my world went dark.

Waking up next to my best friend wasn't the worst thing in the world. It usually meant that a night out on the town had gotten rowdy and we would giggle and groan about the antics from the night before after ordering pizza and taking enough ibuprofen to aid in our recovery. Waking up to your best friend on a hard wood floor next to a pulpit, her still knocked out, while you watched her life force leaving her body for a dark ritual—not as much fun.

The circle had formed again and the chant resumed. I strained to see if I could locate my goblin comrades, but I couldn't see past the circle. The dark, melodious chant left my skin crawling. Thank the gods, I hadn't eaten in hours since my stomach did its best to crawl into my throat. I swallowed, calming the wave of nausea and did a little self-evaluation.

I didn't need to search long. My magic in its entirety had wrapped itself tight within me in an act of self-preservation. The dark magic licked at my skin, but it was either focused on Lola or I needed to write an editorial to *Witch Weekly* singing the praises of magical vaccines. Something to dwell on later.

The number of witches surrounding me was a problem. I strained to hear above the chant, hoping the telltale sound of grunts, thuds, and air crackling that surrounded magical fights. The chant added a white noise cloaking the room, but a sinking feeling in my gut told me the fight had ended, and given that I was lying beaten in the middle of the circle, watching Lola get drained, that didn't bode well for Deval or Vegard.

Tears wanted to form at concern for my friends, but if I was the only one left, I needed to go out fighting and take a few of the bitches with me. My body ached, and I knew from very recent experience that I was not a skilled enough fighter to take on this many people. So I pulled on my magic. *Kingpin first.* They hadn't realized I'd woken.

The thing about surprises was that they only worked once. I needed to blast the woman with everything and pray that I had enough for her son once she was down. After that I didn't really have a plan, but I knew I needed to follow my order of operations, but instead of Please excuse my dear aunt Sally, I'd go Please kill Mommy dearest, her sniveling son, and all the bitches.

I laughed internally at my own terrible joke. It probably meant that I'd reached the appropriate level of crazy necessary to pull this off. On the count of three, I sat up fast. Some cracked ribs seemed to grind in protest, but I'd rather die of a punctured lung than have my soul stolen by this lot. My power rushed forward, hitting the matriarch dead on because she'd been too busy murdering to notice me.

She shrieked. Her people looked down and started toward me, but they stopped when after a shuddering gasp, she called out. "Do not break the circle, you fools. We have too much invested in this one. If we stop the ritual, we all die anyway."

My mind struggled to wrap itself around the fact that as I poured everything that I had into this incredibly powerful witch, and she didn't even bother to lift a finger in retaliation. What did she mean invested? I gritted my teeth and kept pushing magic into her. I saw sweat form on her forehead as her body gave an involuntary shudder, but she kept on chanting.

A minute passed, and my arms began to burn from holding them in front of me as conduits. With all of my training, I'd never had or expected to use a magical attack for such a long period. Short bursts of magic were enough to knock out another caster, and there was no reason for them, but she held on to her cronies' hands for dear life and just kept on trucking while I slowly exhausted myself.

I looked around, confused at what was happening. Then my eyes locked on Lola's magic. It surrounded me, slowly siphoning out of her into the parasites, but I already knew that. The surprise was in the quantity. A cloud of her magic filled the circle the amount and potency ten times that of the average witch, and where Lola had certainly been blessed in many areas, this level of magic was not something she'd ever displayed.

My arms now visibly shook and my T-shirt stuck to my body from the sweat pouring from me. My order of operations was not working as I'd planned. My attack seemed to be hurting me more than it hurt them. I dropped my hands, letting my magic sputter out. I saw a triumphant smile on the woman's face. *Don't get too excited, you old crone.* I studied the cloud of magic around me, a soft pink with hints of purple. The pink I'd recognized. Lola had always given off that shade in her spellwork. The purple added a nice touch, very sparkle princess, but not Lola. It poured from her along with the pink, so using my witch sight I took in the purple and followed it back to its source.

If Lola hadn't been unconscious and open magically from the ritual, I never would have seen what they'd done. Deep in the essence of Lola, in her soul home, a seed had been planted. A weed meant to grow with the witch, harvesting her magic as she grew. These seeds were rare even for dark practitioners because they harvested not only from the victim but also from the caster to keep a seed alive for however long it sat. Given Lola's history with the McAllisters, the weed had been there for over a decade, and now it was time to harvest, or their own field would go fallow.

It's always nice when you can identify obscure spells. Now, there was just the teensy problem of figuring out what to do about it. I'd only read about it briefly at the boot camp and the case study hadn't been such a long-sprouted seed, and even if the weed had only been planted a week ago, I didn't have the equipment or the time let alone the physical capability at the moment to brew a potion to kill it.

I started to despair at losing Lola when a key seemed to turn in my mind, allowing me to think outside of my comfort zone. Lola's power was being pulled out, tethered to the weed. What if I could just pull the weed? Goblins used their planes as magical storage facilities to hold their power for them. Lola obviously wasn't a plane and not my property, but as her best friend for over a decade, I definitely had a claim to her. A click in my own magic home reverberated through me as a door opened in my mind's eye.

Instinctively, I reached for the magic cloud shaky from my own attempt to stop these witches. The minute I touched the magic, the door that had opened became a vacuum, wanting to suck up all of the magic in the air. I pulled back on the door a little, only allowing the purple to enter. I had no problem taking in the weed's power, but I would not take from Lola. My goblin instincts got the hint and began to pull exclusively purple magic from the air.

Initially, it was just a trickle, but as I got the hang of it, it quickly became a wind tunnel of power pouring into me. Apparently a decade of carefully placed magic was even more of a pick-me-up than George. Not that I'd tell him, and I hoped there would never be a repeat. The pain I'd been in moments ago disappeared, replaced by a warm tingling sensation and a heady dose of giddiness. I rose to my feet and let out an elated laugh that sounded as manic as mommy dearest's had earlier. That should have been disconcerting. It wasn't. Neither were the shrieks that began to sound around me.

Instead, I stood in the middle of it all, arms raised in exultation, my head thrown back as I spun around in a circle slowly, never wanting the feeling to end.

"Peg, they're gone. You need to close the door now before it's too late." Deval's steady timbre filled the room.

I didn't want to listen, so I just kept on spinning.

"You are a resilient woman, Peg, and I believe you would survive almost any situation, but I would bet all of my gold that you would not survive the guilt of murdering Lola."

I kept spinning as the words sank in, and just as suddenly my head jerked forward, and I started seeing what Deval spoke of. Sure enough the purple was gone. The McAllisters lay in the circle around me, their bodies husks, drained of magic, and I'd begun to unconsciously pull the cottony pink magic of Lola's magic toward me. I slammed the door slammed shut visualizing a deadbolt locking in place, and a bar dropped down on the door for good measure. I reached for my witch magic, forcing the loose magic again into a cyclone, not for my own hunger this time but to return it to its home. I corralled Lola's magic back into the place the weed had been planted, taking the time to search out any residual malignant magic that could have been left inside of Lola to fester.

Finding nothing, I pushed in the last of the misplaced magic back home. I knelt over my friend and gently shook her shoulder. When that didn't work, I began to lightly tap her face. I didn't want to hurt her, but she needed to wake up and close her soul home. Right now she was easy pickings for a dark practitioner. The longer she stayed open, the more vulnerable she'd become, and the more difficult it would be for her to rebuild her walls.

Deval came and stood behind me. His hand rested on my shoulder for comfort or reassurance or whatever it was he intended. Whatever it was, it felt nice.

Lola finally came to. Sputtering on the floor before curling into fetal position. Heaving sobs came out of her. "Why does it hurt so bad?" she sobbed.

I got down on my knees and rubbed her back. "Lo, love, I know it hurts, but you need to focus. You need to put up your borders. You probably feel like you've been magically gutted, and you sort of were, but you'll feel better once you have it secure again. Can you do that, Lola?"

She whimpered and shook her head. "Can't you do it, Peg? It burns and feels empty at the same time. I don't even know what to do at this point."

I knew that she felt weak in that moment, and she had to be dangerously low power reserves. I grabbed her hand and began to push my magic into her. It was the least I could do, given that I'd unwittingly taken from her in my desperation to stop our enemies.

A gasp sounded from Lola. "That feels so much better. Peg, why does your magic feel different? I'd know yours anywhere, but it feels even more familiar."

"Get your barriers up again, and I'll tell you. You're not gonna like it, but rest assured neither do I. I just hope you'll forgive me at the end of this," I muttered the last sentence because I wasn't sure how Lola would feel about my accidental cannibalization of her magic or my semi-intentional cannibalization of the McAllisters.

Slowly, I fed more and more of my power into Lola, hoping to replace any I'd taken, or at least give her a strong enough boost, so she'd start recharging on her own. Through our connection, her magic became more and more distant from me, in a good way. Lola had been breathing in pained gasps until finally the last magical brick had been placed. She took a deep and steady breath before exhaling and falling from fetal position to being flat on her back.

She looked up at me. "You were right." Her face held no humor just utter defeat and that worried me.

I forced a smile. "There's a first time for everything. You're always saving me. I needed to return the favor. Just two months ago, you talked the vampire lord out of eating me. So really you were due a little assistance."

I'd hoped for a small smile, but all I got was a solemn nod before Lola closed her eyes. "I'm so tired, Peg."

"Then sleep. I won't let anything happen to you."

22

Lola didn't need any more encouragement and went to sleep as though the hard chapel floor was the most luxurious feather bed. Not sure of the injuries she'd sustained magically or otherwise, I frowned, looking down at her fragile form as I stood up. She needed a healer, but that needed to wait. I reached in my pocket, and above all odds, I pulled out my phone still in one piece thanks to an overpriced case.

The battery flashed at me, letting me know that even though I'd managed to save my best friend, my phone's power wasn't long for this world, and just like that, the screen went blank as the phone sang the forlorn death song of its kind, also know as a series of beeps. I let out a soft chuckle. I'd probably have been able to keep it in if I wasn't coming down from a magic high. I shoved the phone back in my pocket and turned to Deval, who'd stayed quietly behind me.

"Any chance you have Pammy's number on speed dial? I almost have her number memorized, but I keep screwing up the last two numbers and calling a Chinese takeout place, and whereas I'm starving, there are a lot of hours left in the night before we are going to get to rest again."

We surveyed the scene around us again before he looked at me. "I'd say that's an accurate assessment. I didn't want to leave you."

I looked up at him, surprised by the emotion coating his voice, and raised a brow. "Getting your ass kicked, too, huh?" I asked trying to make him smile. It didn't work.

"As much as I'm loath to admit it, yes. We needed back up or weapons. We were able to take out one, but it's a miracle that neither Vegard nor I are dead. The death magic they possessed was far greater than I'd expected coming from such a sick-looking people."

I motioned over to Lola. "They had a weed in her. Do you know what those are?"

His eyebrows rose. "A magical curse used to drain another's magic over time but at a high cost in the meantime. How long had it been present?"

I shrugged. "At least a decade. They came to town looking to cash in big time. Pammy had mentioned that they would go to a town and then just as soon as they finished wreaking havoc disappear for years. I don't think they've been able to survive as long as they have off of their average drainings. The true source of their power came from the harvest."

He nodded, taking in my words. "I'd say that is a good hypothesis, but we may never know for sure. Do you know if there were any others?"

"We killed a few earlier tonight. I think we wiped them out, but things like them tend to scurry into some dark place and come back when least expected. Pammy did take some journals and notebooks from them, so hopefully we'll know more soon. Where is Vegard?"

"When we left, he thought he might be able to get

some help that was close, and he went in search of it. I made some calls, and we should have reinforcements arriving soon."

"Can I use that phone now?" I asked as the front door slammed open.

Pammy strode in the room, marching straight for us, her keen sight not missing a thing along her way, which included one dead witch in the back and my personal collection of four dead witch husks up front. She didn't say anything at first, looking at the husks and then me and then back again. Then she did something very un-Pammy. She grasped me in her arms, her soft and steady frame feeling like pure strength despite her being a few inches shorter than me. Then she gave me two smacking kisses, one on each cheek, before taking my face in her hands.

"Sug, I don't know how you did it, but I came in here expecting to find my protégé and all of her friends dead."

If I didn't know better, I'd have said there was a sheen of unshed tears in her eyes. The kind that suggested she had seen some shit, but she shook it off and released me walking a slow circle around the dead.

"This is gonna be a pain in the ass to take care of. Think Bruce'd let us borrow his truck?"

"If you can call him. My phone just died."

She whipped hers out and began to make her phone-tree rounds. I caught bits and pieces: "If you didn't wanna be on trash haul duty, why'd you buy a truck, rookie move…I know your girls want you to read them a bedtime story, but, girl, you're gonna want John to do it….I'll pay you, but it's not every day you see the deadliest coven of drainers killed during their own ritual." She mentioned that last one a few times.

"Everyone's gonna think I'm a freak," I muttered under my breath but not quiet enough.

"No, everyone's gonna think you're a badass, which may be worse."

My eyes rolled to the ceiling. "I'm gonna ask. Why is that worse?"

"You are steadily building a reputation as someone not to be trifled with." Deval broke in for Pammy. "It will bring you more dangerous jobs, high-paying jobs, but it will also bring desperados looking to make a name for themselves at your expense."

"Mhmm." Pammy affirmed.

"Greeeeat. Deval, think you could start spreading rumors around that in actuality I've just had a lucky streak, and I can act like a petulant child if denied caffeine?"

His barked laughter cut through the quiet dim of what would normally be a really cute chapel. "No, that would be worse, I think. Better to stick with the truth. You are a badass."

I flushed a little under the praise but didn't say anything to dispute it, as I'd decided to make it my new mantra. "Well, it's been a while since I've had any caffeine, so we'd better get started because I'm going to crash any moment."

Deval nodded, and we began to do our work. Pammy handed each of us a pair of gloves because Pammy was always prepared. The husks weighed less than I thought they would. Apparently when magic was harvested not much got left behind. It made it difficult to pile the people near the front door since they were fragile. Half of them needed to be swept up with a broom.

Deval had decided that Lola would be more comfortable on one of the padded pews and went to scoop her up when Vegard returned with "backup." He'd chosen the last person I would hace expected. Gregar strode into the room, looking smug and cocky, a broadsword dangling at his side. If I had to guess, I'd say that he hadn't planned on helping but to come in and see the carnage of the aftermath. There was plenty of carnage but not apparently what he'd wanted to see when he saw Michael laid out among the husks, shriveled, dried, and eyeless.

His disbelief and anger shone in his eyes as they darted around the room. Vegard turned and studied his brother. Vegard placed a hand on his Gregar's shoulder, trying to calm him. Gregar brushed his brother's hand aside letting out a battle cry as he pulled his sword, charging the source of his anger. Deval hadn't seen Gregar, but the cry alerted him as he turned around, still holding Lola. As Gregar rushed Deval, his sword ignited with a bright glow of magic. I cried out and tried to push my power forward to block Gregar, but I knew I'd be too late.

Vegard was hot on his heels and grabbed Gregar's shoulder just as he had his sword in a high arc above his head, causing him to spin, sword still in motion. I saw it happening, and so did Deval as he dropped Lola to the floor, bellowing out, "No!"

Gregar's sword, through the worst kind of fate twist, did exactly what he'd intended but to the wrong person as it slid through his brother's neck. Vegard's head fell to the ground with a sickening thud. I held my hand over my mouth as bile rose in my throat. Both Gregar and Deval shouted out. I wanted to think Gregar's was as heart wrenching as Deval's, but he just looked at his brother's lifeless face with rage. Deval stepped over Lola to confront his cousin when the additional reinforcements arrived. Deval's uncle Faxon led the charge.

He took one look at his son's decapitated corpse and held up a shaky hand pointing at Deval. "Murderer." And charged.

Deval parried the older goblin all the while telling the

other goblins present to stand back. I ran to Lola and grabbed her under the arms, dragging her away from where Deval currently grappled with his uncle.

Once she was safe, I looked around the room. Deval managed to put his uncle in a hold.

"Peace, uncle, I did not harm Vegard."

Faxon continued to struggle in the hold his face a bright red as he sputtered nonsensical threats.

I looked around for the actual murderer, sorrow and anger stirring my magic once again and looking for an outlet. Gregar had managed to disappear in the chaos.

The goblins stood back, held there by Griselda, who obeyed her prince. The men and women surrounding her looked uncertain, not knowing what had happened to end Vegard so tragically.

Pammy came and stood by me whispering in my ear, "Justice will be served, Sug. For now we stand aside and don't get involved in this business."

I wanted to yell that we were as deep in this business as anyone else present, but logic held my tongue. A standoff had officially formed, and I didn't think the tension could get any higher. However, it could and it did when, of all people, Delmy Queen of the Goblins entered the room, regal and authoritative taking in the scene. Her gaze lingered on Vegard's head before she looked up to the people gathered.

"Who will speak of these atrocities?"

EPILOGUE

The official invitation to the goblin lair located deep in the heart of the Superstition Mountains, warded and spelled to the hilt, did not bring me any joy. I'd have happily been chauffeured back and forth blindfolded the rest of my days if it meant that Vegard lived. I'd only begun to get to know him, but the end of his life also meant the end of a promising friendship. I tried as I might to focus on my surroundings. Musing that while the Lost Dutchman miner had likely found gold in The Superstitions, the poor man just hadn't realized that it belonged to goblins. Some goblin guard had really screwed the pooch that day.

I felt the corner of my mouth twitch in the beginning of a smile. Guilt halted the movement as I raised my eyes to take in the mourners assembled here in a deep valley at the heart of the mountain. A fissure had been created in the stone where Vegard's body had been propped. His head returned to him, his body in a shroud.

Deval came to stand next to me and whispered in my ear. "Are you thinking of The Lost Dutchman?"

I turned my head and stared up at him. "Of course not. This is a funeral."

His somber gray eyes held just a hint of sparkle. "It is usually an entertaining realization for our guests, and despite this sad affair, if you'd gotten to know Vegard more, you would have known that he enjoyed the lighter elements of life, the whimsy, and the story of a guard off taking a piss while some hillbilly farmer nearly shit himself at the sight of one of our holdings."

I nearly choked on the laughter I held back, though a small squeak did manage to escape. Mourners turned to us, chagrin in their gazes. "Are you trying to get me maimed on my first visit here?" I whispered to Deval.

"They wouldn't touch you. They are all very aware that you are here on the invitation from my mother as well as from me."

"Be that as it may, I'd prefer if they didn't fantasize about maiming me as an alternative to any real aggression."

He inclined his head. "Our ceremony will begin soon. If you would like, you're welcome up front with my mother and me."

I shook my head, giving Deval a shaky smile. "I'd rather be inconspicuous."

"Peg, that is one thing you could never be." With that, he bent down and kissed me in front of his people, in front of his mother. The kiss made my toes curl and warmth spread through me, even as heat flamed my cheeks at the public claim of interest, and I knew that was what it was. He pulled away and gave me a wink before turning to walk up to begin the ceremony.

Lola, who'd been speaking with her family, sidled up next to me and grabbed my hand. I felt a slight shake in it. Cared for by the most talented healers among us, Lola still had a long road to recovery. Building up her magic reserve again would take time, and because her own magical vessel had grown accustomed to a large bit of power the weed had contained, her physical body felt weakened by the lack of it. I let go of her hand and put my arm round her waist. She leaned into me.

I knew Lola hid a tremendous well of guilt over what had happened, but no one blamed her. A magical weed would have influenced her to believe the McAllisters. After everything that had transpired at the chapel, I couldn't deny that I'd been slightly relieved to know that dropping the hos before bros code had outward influence.

We stood there, arms around each other as the sun set over desert mountains, shooting reds, oranges, and pinks across the night sky. A hum went through the crowd, a never-ending steady note began to rise and build as a swarm of earth magic formed, sending vibrations up through our feet and buzzing through the night air. The tone increased in flowing increments, and a crack sounded through the night as the fissure holding Vegard closed, his tomb becoming one of many in the secret valley. Delmy stood before the tomb and took her son's hand.

With my witch sight, I could see that Deval was feeding his mother magic as she carved a symbol in the stone with her index finger that I guessed to now be diamond-hard through her own magic and Deval's. Once it was complete, she turned to her people and raised her hands. The night went silent and still.

The silence was short lived, as Faxon marched forward, his finger pointing accusingly at Deval. "I know he did it, Delmy. I will have my vengeance whether you do the right thing and try him, or I resort to the old ways."

I couldn't see Faxon's face, but Delmy's eyes flashed in the dusk.

"Brother, are you threatening me and spreading poison at your own son's funeral? I do not see your other son, which speaks further to his guilt. I had not wished to do this today, but you have decided to make your play. With Vegard gone, all that is left of your family branch has rotted, and I will not let a branch kill the roots our line. I disavow you and yours from me and mine."

Faxon went still, and he began to sputter. Delmy looked at him with pity, but before he could find any words, she turned and walked away. Deval also walked away, but he came toward me instead of following his mother. She didn't seem bothered by his change of direction. In fact, she looked over at me and briefly let the stone of her face break into a small smile.

As Deval stood with me and Lola in the din, I wasn't sure what freaked me out more: the obvious political and familial upheaval I'd just witnessed or having Deval's mother approve of me.

There we stood in a valley, grief and turmoil filling the air, but I had my best friend on one side, alive and on the mend, my possible goblin soul mate on the other side, and a former goblin duke or whatever they called themselves staring daggers at us. My life continued to get ever more complicated, and I hoped we would all make it past this because as fast as I made new friends, my enemies seemed to grow by the day. Lola squeezed my hand, and I smiled at her. Nope, still more friends than enemies.

ABOUT THE AUTHOR

 Originally from Arizona, I'm currently residing in Chicago, having traded an oven for a freezer. I write Urban Fantasy because I like spooky things. I have a degree in English Literature from Arizona State University and the typical laundry list of jobs that goes with it. When I'm not working the day job or writing, I enjoy eating, reading, watching TV, pretending to be an elf (RPG), coding, and spoiling my cats.

www.ingramcontent.com/pod-product-compliance
Lightning Source LLC
Chambersburg PA
CBHW020323200626
46814CB00006BB/2392